Frank Hird's MERSEYSIDE

Edited and Selected by

Cliff Hayes

**from original stories
by Frank Hird**

BOOK CLEARANCE CENTRE
27-28 Dawson Way, St. John's Precinct, Liverpool, L1 1LH
Tel: 0151 708 5176

This edition published 2005

© BOOK CLEARANCE CENTRE
27-28 Dawson Way, St. John's Precinct,
Liverpool, L1 1LH
Tel: 0151 708 5176

Old Merseyside Tales have been selected from Frank Hird's *Lancashire Stories,* first published c. 1918. Also included are a booklet, *Liverpool 1889,* and *Old Liverpool Pictures.*

The collection was originally compiled by the late Cliff Hayes, to whose memory this reprinted edition is dedicated. Cliff's original introduction to the collection is printed on page 5 of this volume.

Other Book Clearance Centre shops are found at:

Unit 2-8, Fishergate Centre, Preston, PR1 8HJ
Tel: 01772 884846

Unit 6, Marketgate Shopping Centre,
Wigan, WN1 1JS
Tel: 01942 829499

27-28 Dawson Way, St. John's Precinct, Liverpool, L1 1LH
Tel: 0151 708 5176

7, The Mall, Millgate Centre, Bury, BL9 0QQ
Tel: 0161 763 5700

Market Walk, Chorley, PR7 1DE
Tel: 01257 276799

Printed and bound by:
Ashford Colour Press Ltd
Gosport, Hampshire
01329 229700

Foreword

I've been fascinated with Liverpool ever since my Mother told me that it was the biggest port in the world.

The BIGGEST IN THE WORLD... I can still recall the thrill at that — I was about seven at the time — and the fact that MY home town was so important. It somehow rubbed off and I felt I had to tell someone — and promptly **did** as soon as I got back to school. I was associated with THE BIGGEST, which somehow also suggested THE BEST. In the WHOLE WORLD.

That was a long time ago but ever since I've felt a deep local and civic pride and interest. Increasingly I learned of some of Liverpool's stories and legends, from the absence of reference in Domesday — while Walton-on-the-Hill WAS mentioned — to the legendary trials at St. George's Hall, The Maybrick Case, The Wallace Case, and more.

I learned of King John and Liverpool's first charter in the 13th century; of links with the slave trade and the great abolitionists, Roscoe and Huskisson. I found that the great William Gladstone had been a Liverpool man and that the city had so many ''firsts'' that a special book to that effect would be needed — from the first official medical officer of health to the first public wash-houses.

Liverpool is steeped in history and legend, ancient and modern. Her sons and daughters have traversed the world leaving indelible imprints of culture, humour, endeavour. Comics and writers, scientists and sportsmen, politicians, visionaries and entrepreneurs. It was a matter of some regret to me as a youngster that no simple, general history of Liverpool and its characters was available — nothing to tell of the Civil War and the Liver Bird; of the building of the great docks and the tales to flesh the historical skeleton.

Today a whole literature on Liverpool and Merseyside exists and is being expanded constantly. I look to a day when local history becomes part of all local school courses with books like this on the officially recommended reading list. It can only help others enjoy the pride I've enjoyed being a citizen of ''The Biggest Port In The World''.

I hope it does, because it has already enriched me. Despite being a student — for want of a better word — of Liverpool stories and history for most of my life, this book has given me more. More stories and more details to bring to life the times and events of my Merseyside ancestors. Cliff Hayes and his team must be congratulated on a job well done in researching the tales, having found them first and adding an extra dimension to Liverpool's library. I thought it was a book to browse through — to dip into for half an hour perhaps at bedtime. I found it so fascinating, however, that it has become a long, solid read instead. I just wish it had been out years ago.

Bob Azurdia died on 23 July, 1991.
This introduction is to his memory.

Original Foreword

FROM whatever point of view it may be approached—topographical, archæological, commercial or romantic — no county possesses so varied a history as Lancashire.

Lancashire has had many historians, such as Whitaker, Baines, Harland and Whatton. There is a literature, dealing with the county from every aspect, which fills many pages in the British Museum catalogue. But, although the greatest pains in research have been taken to ensure historical accuracy, *Lancashire Stories* does not claim to be a history. It may be described as the result of a consideration of the history of the county entirely from the human point of view ; and, that there should be variety and constant change of interest, no order of dates has been followed. Human nature is the same to-day as it was in the days of the Normans ; the story has been the one object of the writer, not the period.

It has been suggested that a bibliography should be printed with this work, but in a publication destined for the general reader, rather than for the historian and archæologist, such a list would be out of place. The authorities are given in the text wherever it has been deemed essential to the interest and value of the story.

Ready and most courteous help has been extended to me by the Lancashire libraries in the search for material and for illustrations to these stories. All the books, old prints, etc., in their possession were freely placed at my disposal, permission at the same time being given for photographs to be taken of anything germane to my purpose. My warm thanks are therefore due for this valuable assistance to Mr. A. E. Sutton, of the Manchester Reference Library ; Mr. George T. Shaw, of the Liverpool Reference Library ; Mr. R. J. Gordon, of the Rochdale Public Library ; Mr. Charles Madeley, of the Warrington Public Library ; Mr. Charles Leigh, of Owens College Library, Manchester ; Mr. J. N. Dowbiggin, of the Public Library, Storey Institute, Lancaster, and to the Harris Free Library, Preston and Mr. James Brockbank, of the *Manchester Courier*, and Mr. J. L. Edmondson, of the Manchester *Daily Mail*, for their valuable suggestions.

My acknowledgments are specially due to the London Library and its assistants.

FRANK HIRD.

Introduction

Liverpool Daily Post and Echo

I have, for a long time, tried to find a book of stories, tales or myths of Lancashire. A book that was not a long history or just the bare facts, but one of the unusual, and of the characters of what is the most fascinating county in England. After much searching and help from the Second Hand trade I came across a 900 page bulky volume "Lancashire Stories" by Frank Hird, written about 1918 and very popular at the time, It was just right, it had just the story tellers feel that I was looking for. It was informative, and factually correct but not over long. Tony Gibb first showed me the book and it was on his suggestion I first read it.

Having costed out a reprint of the 2 volumes the cost, even in paperback would have been £10.00 a copy, so it was reluctantly put on a shelf and left in abeyance, although I still found myself dipping into it on many occasions, as I found it fascinating.

I then decided to try again and approach the project with the same plan as with "Lancashire 150 Years Ago" and split up the county into three. I took the book again, and for weeks was up at the crack of dawn and every weekend, and read and re-read the 600 pages. Each Saturday morning I would switch on Radio Merseyside and listen to Gerry Philips while I edited and made notes to check out some of the facts. Listening to the news items and features made me think that this book was the news items and features from the past 250 years. It had just the feel of local radio in giving the interesting details and facts to fill out the stories.

So here is the Merseyside section, edited just a little, and presented, hoping that you agree that Frank Hird wrote them in a style that makes for good, informative and interesting reading.

Very little is known about Frank Hird other than that he lived in the Merseyside area, it is thought on the edge of the City of Liverpool and that this was the only book he wrote. But I for one am grateful he did write it and I hope you agree we have produced an interesting and informative book.

Cliff Hayes

P.S. Please remember that they were written in approximately 1910 so if it refers to 40 years ago, it refers to 1870. If the story states 100 years ago then it means 1810 etc...

Contents

THE OLD CUSTOM HOUSE AT LIVERPOOL

THE old Custom House at Liverpool stood at the east side of Old Dock. Writing of it in 1812, a "Stranger in Liverpool" says that "it was a plain, and for its size a convenient, structure," but that "as a dock was made, proves the existence of a pool or haven near the place which it occupies, as the land granted for the making of the dock was said "to be in or near a certain place called the 'pool' on the south side of the said town of Liver-

THE OLD CUSTOM HOUSE, LIVERPOOL

commercial building it is in every way unworthy the character of a town so justly distinguished for the splendour and convenience of its public edifices." The Old Dock was the first dock to be constructed in Liverpool under the authority of an Act of Parliament obtained in 1710. A paragraph in the Act, under which this pool." It was 195 yards in length, and varied in breadth from 90 yards at the broadest part to 70 yards at the narrowest. The gates were 33 feet wide and 25 deep —an interesting comparison with the leviathan dock gates of Liverpool to-day. It was used by West India ships, Irish traders, and vessels from the Mediter-

7

ranean. In the Old Custom House a flight of steps led through a small arcade into an open vestibule or piazza, under which were the entrances into the different offices below stairs. On the floor above was the Long Room where the business of the Customs was transacted. The building was of brick with two wings, having at the back a large yard with warehouses. But in 1812 this building was already too small for the increasing requirements of Liverpool trade, and the Stranger says: "It is intended to erect a new one on a very extensive and commodious plan by the authority of an Act of Parliament which empowers the trustees to fill up the Old Dock and appropriate a part of this site to that purpose." In the course of time this was done, and the present superb building, which has been described as " one of the most magnificent pieces of architecture that our age has produced and (which) deserves to rank even with St. Paul's and with other works of the first order," was erected.

The new Custom House with its superb Ionic portico facing the river was built by the Liverpool Corporation, but was afterwards bought by the Government for £150,000.

APPRENTICES' HOLIDAYS

SIX weeks' holiday in the year would appear beyond the bounds of possibility to the Lancashire apprentice of to-day, yet they were enjoyed by his forbears in the eighteenth century. In an agreement drawn up in 1790, between the trustees of the Liverpool Bluecoat Hospital and Mr. James Meredith, for the apprenticeship of two hundred boys to the trade of pin-making for eleven years, it was stipulated and agreed that they should have the following holidays—

Christmas, fourteen days.
Good Friday.
Easter, two afternoons, and from three o'clock the third day.
Whitsuntide, the same.
Shrove Tuesday.
Ash Wednesday.
Conversion of St. Paul, Jan. 25.
King Charles's Martyrdom, Jan. 30.
Purification, Feb. 2.
St. Matthew's Day, Feb. 24.
Annunciation (Lady Day), March 25.
St. Mark's Day, April 25.

St. Philip and St. James's Day, May 1 (May Day).
Ascension Day (Holy Thursday).
Restoration of King Charles II. (Royal Oak Day), May 29.
St. Barnabas' Day, June 11.
St. John the Baptist's Day (Midsummer Day), June 24.
St. James's Day (Liverpool Summer Fair), July 25.
St. Bartholomew's Day, Aug. 24.
St. Matthew's Day, Sept. 21.
St. Michael's Day (Michaelmas Day), Sept. 29.
Liberty Day.
St. Luke's Day, Oct. 18.
Anniversary of the King's Inauguration.
St. Simon and St. Jude's Day, Oct. 28.
All Saints' Day, Nov. 1.
Gunpowder Plot (Guy Fawkes's Day), Nov. 5.
Martinmas Day (Liverpool Winter Fair), Nov. 11.
St. Andrew's Day, Nov. 30.
St. Thomas's Day, Dec. 21.

TOXTETH PARK

TOXTETH PARK, the famous suburb of Liverpool, was formerly a deer park belonging to the Earls and Dukes of Lancaster, passing into the possession of the Molyneux family in the reign of Henry VI., when Sir Richard Molyneux was granted the chief forestership of " the Royal Forests and Parks in the wapentake of West Derbyshire, with the offices of serjeant or steward of that and the wapentake of Salfordshire, and Constable of the Castle of Liverpool," to himself and his male heirs for ever. The forest of Simonswood and the two royal parks of Croxteth and Toxteth remained in the possession of the Molyneux family until early in the nineteenth century, when they were divided into allotments for building purposes. Writing of Toxteth Park, in 1817, Matthew Gregson, one of Lancashire's most learned antiquarians, says that so late as the year 1770, Toxteth Park was entirely composed of farms; in that year the first farm was broken up for building land. In 1802 there were 352 houses at Toxteth Park, inhabited by 2,609 people; in 1811 the houses had increased to 1280, and the inhabitants to 5,864. " Of all the villages and townships surrounding Liverpool," says Gregson, " none is more closely connected with it than Toxteth Park. Washed by the Mersey after it has passed the town, it is one of the most pleasant and healthy spots in the vicinity of Liverpool." A "delightful retreat " in Toxteth Park in 1817 was Knot's Hole, famed for its dingle which had been made by the drying up of a stream. A local poet, with quaint conceit, thus describes the disappearance of the stream—

INSCRIPTION ON THE VALE OR DINGLE
AT KNOT'S HOLE.

Stranger that with careless feet
Wanderest thro' this green retreat,
Where, near gently-bending slopes,
Soft the distant prospect opes;

Where the fern, in fringèd pride,
Decks the lovely valley's side;
Where the linnet chirps his song,
Flitting as thou tread'st along;

Know, where now thy footsteps pass
O'er the bending tufts of grass,
Bright gleaming thro' the encircling
     wood,
Once a Naiad rolled her flood.

If her Urn, unknown to fame,
Pour'd no far-extended stream,
Yet along its grassy side,
Clear and constant flow'd the tide.

Grateful for the tribute paid,
Lordly Mersey lov'd the maid:
Yonder rocks still mark the place
Where she met his stern embrace.

Stranger, curious would'st thou learn,
Why she mourns her wasted Urn?
Soon a short and simple verse
Shall her hapless fate rehearse.

Ere yon neighbouring spires arose,
That the upland prospect close,
Or ere along the startled shore
Echoed loud the cannon's roar,

Once the maid in summer's heat
Careless left her cool retreat,
And by sultry heat opprest,
Laid her wearied limbs to rest

Forgetful of her daily toil
To trace each tract of humid soil,
From dews and bounteous show'rs to
     bring
The limpid treasure of her spring;

Enfeebled by the scorching ray
She slept the circling hours away;
And when she op'd her languid eye,
Found her silver Urn was dry.

Heedless Stranger, who so long
Hast listen'd to an idle song,
Whilst trifles thus thy notice share,
Hast thou no URN that asks thy care?

MRS. HARDMAN OF ALLERTON

THE lady who was the subject of the following obituary notice, which is frequently quoted, was the wife of James Hardman of Rochdale, whose brother, John Hardman, was a Liverpool merchant and member of Parliament for that city. The two brothers bought Allerton Hall, a house that was afterwards famous as the residence of William Roscoe, the celebrated banker and literary man, who was one of the founders of the Liverpool Athenæum, and who was largely instrumental in the creation of other public institutions in that city towards the close of the eighteenth century. A curious legal position arose after the death of James Hardman in 1759. Allerton appears to have been vested in the two brothers, James Hardman, who survived the member of Parliament, becoming sole owner. John Hardman had died childless. James Hardman had three sons and a daughter, who all died before they came of age, and at his death it was discovered that such a contingency as the death of all four children had not been contemplated by the two brothers in drawing up the settlement of the property. The outcome of this was litigation for many years amongst the Hardman next of kin. This is the notice—

" On Thursday the twelfth of February 1795, died at Allerton in the county of Lancaster, in the ninety-third year of her age, Mrs. Jane Hardman widow of the late James Hardman Esq. of Rochdale, sister-in-law of John Hardman Esq. formerly representative in parliament for the borough of Liverpool, and daughter of George Leigh Esq. of Oughtrington. On the death of her husband she was left with a hopeful family of three sons, who nearly arrived at manhood, and one daughter who died at an early age. Deprived of her own offspring, her affections embraced a wider circle, and for a long time she was a resource to the unfortunate, and a blessing to her friends. Her charities were as judicious as they were liberal ; when large, not lavish, when small, not promiscuous. To approach her was to partake of her bounty. She possessed good sense without austerity ; true religion without intolerance ; her indulgence was for others, her severity for herself. A life of temperance and virtue secured to her an old age of cheerfulness and respectability, and enabled her to wait the close of her days with fortitude and resignation.

" When virtue nipt in early bloom
  Untimely from the world retires,
With just regret we mourn the doom
  That blasts the hope which youth inspires.

" But when to virtue's arduous task
  Extended length of days is given,
The work complete, no more we ask,
  But yield the ripen'd fruit to heaven."

LIVERPOOL AND THE ARMADA

THE first definite news which reached Queen Elizabeth and her advisers of the sailing of the mighty Armada which Philip II. collected together in the ports of Spain, wherewith to utterly crush the English people, and place their country under the dominion of Rome, was brought by a Liverpool merchant named Humphrey Brooke. According to his statement Brooke left St. Jean de Luz the day after one of the many portions of the Armada sailed from Bilbao to join the rest of that mighty fleet. Treachery must have been at work, otherwise Humphrey Brooke could not have supplied the items upon the "particular note" he sent with such patriotic haste to the Queen's ministers, and which was as follows—

"The particular notes of the King of Spain his fleet, departed out of Biscay and the province the 13th of August, whereof is General Don John Martinas de Realde, natural of the town of Bilbao.

Imprimus, VIII armados or great ships of VII and VIII hundred tons the piece.

Item, IIII reserves of small ships of the burden of 60, 70, and 80 tons.

Item, VI small barks made gally wise that row 30 oars upon a side.

Item, 2000 mariners.

Item, 4000 soldiers.

Item, 20,000 calivers.

Item, 20,000 muskets.

Item, 1000 Quintals of powder.

Item, 20,000 long pikes for horsemen.

Item, 78,000 Quintals of biscuit.

Item, 100 tons of garlic.

Item, 20,000 porkers for victuals.

Item, 3000 Quintals of Holland fish.

Item, the King's commission sealed up, not to be opened before they were 30 leagues at sea.

Item, the common speech of the vulgar people was that they did go either to Ireland, or else to Rochelle, but the opinion of the most was that they went for Ireland.

By me Humphrey Brooke of Liverpoole, Merchant, departed out of St. Jean de Luz in France, the day after that the fleet set sail from the passage to go along the coast to meet the rest of the fleet which was incastred."

TREACLE=DIPPING AT SOUTHPORT

A SPORT that caused much amusement at Southport in old days was treacle-dipping. A large dish was placed upon a table which stood upon a platform, so that the spectators could have a good view. A quantity of treacle was poured into the dish until it was about three or four inches in depth; then some shillings and sixpences were thrown in. The rule was that the coins could only be taken out of the treacle by the teeth of the competitors, and, whether they were successful or not, when they emerged from the sticky mass, their faces were wiped with feathers, to the great delight of the watching crowd.

LIVERPOOL'S FIRST MEMBERS OF PARLIAMENT

LIVERPOOL was represented in the first English Parliament ever called by writ. This was in 1296, when Edward I., sorely pressed for money, summoned the representatives of the boroughs of the kingdom and knights of the shires to a parliament at Westminster. Liverpool sent "two honest and discreet burgesses," Adam Fitz-Richard and Robert Pinklowe, who thus were amongst those representatives of their fellow-countrymen who passed the statute which is known as "*De tallagio non sum cedendo*," which first established the principle that Parliament must control the finances of the kingdom, and not, as heretofore, leave them practically at the disposal of the Sovereign.

Nothing, unfortunately, has come down to us concerning these first members of Parliament for Liverpool; all that we know is that they were paid their travelling expenses, and wages for their services at Westminster, which goes to show that the members of the first English Parliament received payment. When Edward II. succeeded his father in 1306, a new Parliament was summoned, to which Liverpool sent Richard More and John More as its representatives. From that time no further writs were issued to the town for two hundred and forty years.

The reason why writs for two members of Parliament should be issued to a place which only numbered eight hundred and forty inhabitants has been frequently discussed, but it would seem the answer lies in the fact that Liverpool was considered as a place of great promise, for, whilst acting as regent for his brother King Richard Cœur de Lion, the attention of John—afterwards King Lackland—had been called to the advantageous site of Liverpool as a port. When he succeeded to the throne he visited Lancashire. This was in 1206. There are records of his being at Lancaster, and at Chester, in February of that year, and although there is no record of his passing through Liverpool, his keen interest in the place may be taken as evidence of such a visit, especially as it lay immediately on his road between the capitals of the two counties. In the following year King John exchanged a property called the English Lea, with Henry Fitzwarine, of Lancaster, for Liverpool. The document of exchange was signed by the King at Winchester, being witnessed by a number of earls and barons, and countersigned by the Archdeacon of Wells. At the same time and place John signed the charter which made his newly-acquired property a borough. The following is the translation of King John's charter, which was in Latin—

"The King, to all who may be willing to have burgages at the town of Liverpul etc. Know ye that we have granted to all who shall take burgages at Liverpul, that they should have all liberties and free customs in the town of Liverpul which any free borough on the sea hath in our land. And we command you that securely and in our peace you may come there to receive and inhabit our burgages, and in testimony hereof we transmit to you these our letters patent. Witness Simon de Pateshill at Winchester, the 28th day of August in the ninth of our reign."

The burgages referred to were tenements or dwellings which must have been built by King John before he granted the charter.

Twenty-two years later, John's son, Henry III., gave Liverpool a new charter (1229), which is very significant of the growth of the place. King John had offered his burgages, to all those who chose to settle at Liverpool, on the widest principles of free trade ; all alike were to have liberties and free customs. But the burgesses already in possession appear to have shown considerable anxiety to introduce a protectionist clause into their new charter, for in that of Henry he enacted that the burgesses of the borough should have a merchant's guild with a meeting house where they might transact their business (this was called a *Hanse*), that only the members of this guild should have free customs, and " that no one who is not of the same guild shall transact any merchandise in the said borough, unless by consent of the same burgesses."

When Henry's son, Edward I., succeeded to the throne, in 1272, the wars in which he was perpetually engaged reduced him to the most serious financial embarrassments, to remedy which he was obliged to resort to extraordinary and illegal measures. One of these was the issue of writs to test the validity of titles to land held by corporations and private individuals. Wherever the least flaw could be found in a title-deed Edward promptly seized the property as Lord Paramount. The inquiries in Lancashire were held by Hugh de Cressingham, the King's treasurer, who, a few years later, made himself so detestable to the Scotch that after the battle of Stirling (September 1297) they flayed his dead body and cut the skin into strips. De Cressingham held his court in the octave of the Holy Trinity, that is during the month of June 1292, at Lancaster, and here the bailiffs and commonalty of Liverpool were summoned to appear, to show by what warrant they claimed to be quit of certain tolls and taxes which belonged to the crown " without the license and will of the Lord the King, or of his progenitors." It is recorded that " certain men of the borough of Liverpool came for the commonalty, and say that they have not at present a bailiff of themselves, but have been accustomed to have until Edmund, the King's brother (Edmund, first Earl of Lancaster, son of Henry III.) impeded them, and permitted them not to have a free borough, wherefore at present they do not claim the aforesaid liberties except that they may be quit of common fines and amercements of the county etc., and of toll, stallage, etc., throughout the whole kingdom." Toll, lastage, passage, pontage, and stallage were moneys exacted from traders and merchants for the taking in and putting out of ballast, passing rivers, crossing bridges, or exposing goods for sale. The burgesses of Liverpool were specially exempted from these dues all over the kingdom by the charter of Henry III.

The " certain men " complained that Edmund, the King's brother, had deprived them of the liberties and privileges which had been conferred upon them by his grandfather and his father. Hugh de Cressingham and his court decreed that " whereas it appears by their evidence that the aforesaid Edmund hath usurped and occupied the aforesaid liberties, the sheriff is commanded that he cause him to come here on Monday next, to answer for himself."

Notwithstanding the summons of the King's commissioners to appear before them, no action was taken against the Earl for his usurpation of the rights of Liverpool. This was probably due to the fact that he was the King's brother. He took the tolls for forty years afterwards.

"THE CHILDE OF HALE"

IN the church of Hale is a gravestone with this inscription: "Here lyeth the bodye of John Middleton, the Chylde of Hale. Born A.D. 1578. Dyed A.D. 1623." This "Chylde of Hale" was a famous giant, nine feet three inches in

THE CHILDE OF HALE AND THE
KING'S WRESTLER

height, whose hand was seventeen inches long, and the breadth of his palm eight and a half inches. During the eighteenth century his body was disinterred, and for some time the principal bones were kept at Hale Hall, but were afterwards re-buried. The "Childe's" thighbone reached from an ordinary man's hip to his feet, and the remainder of the skeleton was in proportion. His strength was prodigious, and so great became his fame that Sir Gilbert Ireland of Hale Hall took him to the Court of James I., where, to do honour to their native county some Lancashire gentlemen accoutred him with much magnificence, "with large ruffs about his neck and hands, a striped doublet of crimson and white; round his waist a blue girdle embroidered with gold; large white plush breeches powdered with blue flowers; green stockings; broad shoes of a light colour, having red heels, and tied with large bows of red ribbon; just below his knees bandages of the same colour, with large bows; by his side a sword, suspended by a broad belt over his shoulder, and embroidered, as his girdle, with blue and gold, with the addition of gold fringe upon the edge." In this gorgeous raiment he is said to have wrestled with the King's wrestler, whom he easily conquered, putting out the man's thumb.

There is no record of what happened to the "Childe's" clothes during the wrestling bout, but it is to be imagined that the "large ruffs," and the "striped doublet of crimson and white," and the "blue girdle embroidered with gold," must have suffered considerably. His victory, however, was not popular, and so displeased were some of the courtiers by the injury done to the King's wrestler, that James dismissed the "Childe" with a present of £20. On his homeward journey to Hale, the "Childe" stopped for some time at Brasenose College, Oxford, where there were many Lancashire students, and it was whilst he was there that the life-size portrait of him, which still hangs in the library of that college, was painted.[1]

The most amazing stories were told of

[1] The sketch is from a photograph of this portrait, taken by the kind permission of the Bursar and Fellows of Brasenose College.

14

the origin of his giant stature, and his feats of strength. It was said that he had grown to his great height and bulk in a single night in consequence of spells and incantations practised upon him. Another story says, "There exists a cavity in the sands near Hale in Lancashire, where tradition asserts that, on one occasion the famous 'Childe' fell asleep, and on awaking found all his clothes had burst, and so much had he grown during this short nap that he doubted his own identity. On his way homewards he was attacked by a furious bull; but so strong had he become that he caught it by the horns and threw it to an immense distance. The bull did not approve of such tossing, and, consequently, suffered him to proceed without further molestation."

A still more extravagant tradition shows the popular belief in the "Childe's" preternatural strength. "He was so strong in one of his illnesses that his friends had to chain him in bed. When he recovered, two of the chains were given away : one was sent to Chester to keep the Dee Mills from floating down the river; the second was sent to Boston to prevent the Stump from being blown into the sea. And the third was lent in order to chain down his infernal majesty, who had been captured when suffering from an internal complaint."

The "Childe" could only stand upright in the centre of the cottage in which he lived with his mother. Some robbers, it is said, tried to break into the cottage on one occasion. They had removed a window and were about to enter when they were confronted by the "Childe"; so terrified were they by what they believed to be an apparition that they took to their heels and never looked behind them till they reached the shore of the Mersey at Liverpool.

A descendant of the "Childe's" family, Charles Chadwick, was living in 1804 and was over six feet in height.

"THE BONNY GRAY"

EDWARD, twelfth Earl of Derby, who died in 1834, was passionately fond of cock-fighting. This song, which is taken from an old ballad-sheet, shows that the cock-fight which it describes took place at the cockpit in Liverpool, and that whilst Lord Derby and the Prescot lads backed the cock called "Charcoal Black," the Liverpool lads supported the bird named "Bonny Gray," which proved the victor—

Come all you cock-merchants far and near,
Did you hear of a cock-fight happening here?
Those Liverpool lads, I've heard them say,
'Tween the Charcoal Black and the Bonny Gray.

We went to Jim Ward's,[1] and he called for a pot
Where this grand cock-battle was fought,
For twenty guineas a-side these cocks did play,
The Charcoal Black and the Bonny Gray.

Then Lord Derby came swaggering down,
"I'll bet ten guineas to a crown,
If this Charcoal Black he gets fair play,
He'll clip the wings of your Bonny Gray."

Now when the cocks came to the sod,
Cry the Liverpool lads, "How now? What odds ?"
"The odds," the Prescot lads did say,
"'Tween the Charcoal Black and the Bonny Gray."

This cock-fight was fought hard and fast,
Till Black Charcoal he lay dead at last.
The Liverpool lads gave a loud huzza,
And carried away the Bonny Gray.

[1] A prize-fighter who kept an inn at Liverpool.

LIVERPOOL AND THE SLAVE TRADE

ENGLAND first began to trade with Africa in the reign of Queen Elizabeth, who in the year of the Armada (1588) limited the trade to a company under letters patent, which were renewed both by James I. and Charles I. Shortly after Charles II. was restored to the throne, the Dutch having harried and robbed some of the ships engaged in this trade, he gave a charter to a body of merchants which was called "The Company of Royal Adventurers of England to Africa," the object being apparently that the ships might sail together for protection. But this company speedily got into difficulties, and resigned its charter to another company which was formed under the name of the "Royal African Asiento Company." Asiento is the Spanish word for a contract or undertaking.

This company in 1689 entered into a contract to supply the Spanish West Indies with slaves. Their charter was taken away in the reign of William and Mary, but it made no difference to the company, which not only carried on its hideous traffic as heretofore, but seized the ships of private traders. At Kingston in Jamaica they had a dépôt to which they sent the unfortunate negroes they captured in Africa. It was called the Southsea House. Although the monopoly of the slave traffic had been taken away from the Asiento Company in 1689, and declared illegal, they continued to exercise it for nine years longer, in spite of a determined effort on the part of some Bristol merchants. In 1698 "the trade was thrown open," and from 1701 to 1709 fifty-seven Bristol ships were employed in carrying slaves from Africa to the Windward Isles and Virginia. Liverpool at the time had no inducement to enter into the slave trade, as she was busily engaged in carrying Manchester goods to Jamaica, whence they were smuggled as contraband into the Spanish possessions. But in 1709 a barque of thirty tons burden made the venture, and carried fifteen slaves from Africa to the West Indies—the first instance that is known of Liverpool engaging in the slave trade.

When the monopoly was taken away from the Asiento Company it was enacted by Parliament that private traders should pay the company ten per cent. for the repairs of the forts and the expenses of the factories in Africa. The word factories was used to describe the slave dépôts. Endless quarrels and disputes resulted from this enactment, and finally Parliament, wearied by petitions and counter-petitions, granted a sum of money for this up-keep, decreeing that all persons trading to Africa should pay to the chamberlain of London, or the clerk of the Merchants' Hall, Bristol, or to the town clerk of Liverpool, forty shillings for the freedom of the new company, which was to consist of all the King's subjects trading between Cape Blanco and the Cape of Good Hope. Three committee-men were to be sent alike from London, Bristol and Liverpool, the nine having the management of the business, and the charge of the forts and factories.

This decision of Parliament threw open the slave trade to any who cared to pay forty shillings "for the freedom of the new company"; and immediately upon its promulgation Liverpool sent fifteen ships of an average burden of seventy-five tons each. Seven years later the number was thirty-three, and in 1751 it had risen to fifty-three—and ships of a largely increased tonnage. It must be remembered that the tonnage of the wooden sailing-ships of the eighteenth century represents a considerable difference in size in the same figures as applied to the iron vessels of to-day. From this year of the fifty-three vessels engaged in what was tactfully called the "African trade," the nauseous traffic increased by leaps and bounds until it became one of the most profitable sources of commerce to the quickly growing port.

The voyages of the slave-ships had a treble advantage. On the outward journey to the West Coast of Africa they carried Manchester goods and a variety of other articles, which they sold profitably on their arrival. Then they shipped the public opinion upon a community. In the year 1788 it was stated that out of the sixty thousand slaves carried from West Africa each year, half that number were taken in Liverpool ships, bringing a profit of thirty thousand pounds to the merchants of the town. It was in this year that the suppression of the trade began to be agitated, but until that time its horror and enormity seemed to have occurred to no one save a few Quakers.

LIVERPOOL IN 1680

slaves from the dépôts—"factories"—into which the unfortunate beings had been collected by the slave-dealers who "worked the interior," and carrying them to the West Indies or America, sold them either direct to the planters or in the open market. With the proceeds of this barter of human flesh and blood, these Liverpool mariners brought back cargoes of sugar and rum. So their voyages brought in a triple profit. In our own day and generation such a proceeding, unless carried out by men of the most debased type, is inconceivable ; but in the Liverpool of the late eighteenth century, merchants of the highest standing engaged in the trade—kind-hearted, benevolent and honourable men, who wittingly would have done no man an injury. An interesting example this, of the effect of

The slaves were considered wholly and solely as cargo, as the following bill of lading of a slave-ship shows :—

Shipped by the grace of God in good order and well-conditioned, by Irving and Fraser, in and upon the good snow called the *Byam*, whereof is master under God for this present voyage, George Martin, and now riding at anchor in the Rispongo, and by God's grace bound for the West Indies ; to say two hundred and eight slaves, being marked and numbered as in the margin ; and are to be delivered in the like good order and well-conditioned at the aforesaid port of West Indies, the danger of the sea, mortality and insurrection only excepted—unto order or their assigns. Freight for the slaves paid, vessel belonging to the owners, with primage and average accustomed. In witness whereof the master and the purser of the said ship hath affirmed to three bills of lading, all of this tenor and date; one of which bills being accomplished, the other two to stand void; and so God send the good ship to her desired port in safety. Amen. Dated in Kissing 14 May 1803.

GEORGE MARTIN.

In the margin are these figures—

Men	. . . .	97
Women	. . .	39
Boys	. . . .	44
Girls	. . . .	25
		205
Died	. . . .	3
		208
Shipped	. . .	

And not only were the slaves sold in the West Indies; they were actually sold in Liverpool itself. In 1765, this advertisement appeared :—

To be sold by auction at George's Coffee House betwixt the hours of six and eight, a very fine negro girl about eight years of age, very healthy, and hath been some time from the coast. Any person wishing to purchase the same may apply to Capt. Robert Syers, at Mr. Bartley Hodgetts, Mercer and Draper, near the Exchange, where she may be seen till the time of sale.

In the following year, Williamson's *Advertiser* announced :—

To be sold
At the Exchange Coffee House, in Water Street, this day the 12th inst. September, at one o'clock precisely
Eleven negroes
Exported per the *Angola*.
Broker.

It will doubtless be a surprise to many to learn that slaves were actually owned in England, but such was the case until the year 1772, and the abolition of this blot on our civilization was entirely owing to Granville Sharp, a philanthropist and writer.

In 1765, Sharp had befriended a negro called Jonathan Strong, whom he found starving in the streets, and abandoned by his master, a man called David Lisle. Two years later Lisle had the negro thrown into prison as a runaway slave; but Sharp succeeded in obtaining his release and prosecuted Lisle for assault and battery. Lisle then brought an action against Sharp for unlawfully detaining the property of another. All the great legal luminaries of the kingdom declared against Sharp, confirming a judgment given some forty years previously that masters had property in their slaves even when in England. But, nothing daunted, Sharp interested himself in cases similar to that of Jonathan Strong, and in 1772, in advocating the cause of a negro called John Somerset, obtained the memorable decision—which was the first victory in the struggle for the emancipation of slaves— "that as soon as any slave sets foot upon English territory he becomes free."

As an instance of the difference between the point of view of to-day and that of the eighteenth century, it may be mentioned that John Newton, the celebrated rector of St. Mary Woolnoth in the City of London, actually studied for the ministry whilst in command of a Liverpool slave-ship.

THE LOST FARM

A Legend of Southport

LONG before the earliest beginnings of Southport there stood, close to the flat sandy shore, a ruined and deserted farm-house. Time had rotted the thatch upon the old house and upon the barn near by. The garden and the few acres of pasture-land were covered with sand, which had also drifted high against the broken and weather-stained walls. Each year the mounds of sand grew higher, the coarse grass which covered them not only binding them together but holding all the fresh sand that was thrown from the shore. And there came a day when nothing but a large hummock marked the site of what had been a human dwelling-place. To the few fisher-folk, who then were the only inhabitants of the brilliant health resort of to-day, this desolate spot became known as "The Lost Farm."

But years before the sand had finally engulfed the ruins of the old farm, and blotted out the acres of scanty pasture, a curious story had been told of its last inhabitants ; a story that lost nothing in the telling, and which clung to the place during several generations. Roby has preserved the story in his *Traditions of Lancashire.*

George Grimes, the last occupant of the farm, was half-fisherman, half-farmer, selling the produce of his nets either amongst the neighbouring gentry or, together with the produce of his land, at Ormskirk market. For a man in his position he was reputed to be passing rich. At any rate he was sufficiently well off to be able to afford the luxury of a servant. When the story opens this place was held by a tall, dark-browed young man of athletic build, who had been recommended to Grimes by a Roman Catholic gentleman in the neighbourhood

some twelve months previously. This servant's name was Dick, and although he could hear all that was said to him, he could only answer by signs or by writing. He was dumb. Whether he had been born thus afflicted, or whether he had lost the power of speech, was unknown. The man was a mystery. Whence he came, what was his past history, whether he had friends or family—all alike were unknown. He made his meaning clear by rough sketches and drawings with chalk upon the floor or the table, a method of communication regarded with so much disfavour by the superstitious fisher-folk round about that they became convinced he had direct dealings with Satan.

When Dick, or "Dummy" as he was sometimes called, first entered Grimes's service he was so ignorant of all the duties appertaining to the situation that only the lowness of his wages prevented the old man sending him away. Grimes was a miser, and finding his new servant both apt to learn and diligent, he kept him, with the result that in a short while not only was Dick thoroughly conversant with the work on the little farm, but "could unreef a sail or make a net with the best labourer in the parish."

It was Grimes's beautiful daughter, Katherine, who had taught the dumb man to make nets, as well as to knit ; where to find the best peats, and the best way of snaring rabbits. The two spent many hours together, and as Katherine had been at some pains to learn the signs by which he expressed himself, they were able to "talk" without difficulty.

One day when a spell of stormy weather had reduced the house supplies, Grimes and Dick went down to the sea-shore with the intention of catching a few fish for the mid-day meal. But to

Grimes's rage and consternation his boat was gone. A storm of oaths and objurgations fell upon Dick, whom Grimes accused of having fastened the boat so carelessly that she had slipped her anchor. In the midst of his upraidings, however, he spied the little vessel sailing towards the shore, with a stranger in its stern. The boat ran upon the sandy beach, the stranger stepped out and was about to walk away when the angry owner stopped him with—

"Holloa, friend! Your disposition be freer than welcome methinks. Holloa, I say, whither away so fast?"

But the stranger paid no attention, and walked on. Grimes, however, was not the man to accept such treatment lightly, and hurrying after him brought him to a standstill. There was a brief parley, which ended in Grimes's indignation at the use of his boat being mollified by a piece of gold. Nevertheless he was curious to know the reason of the stranger taking his boat out and sailing back again; it was perplexing, seeing the rough sea and the high wind. But all the answer he received was—

"Seek not to know; 'tis a doomed thing and accursed. I would have given thrice my revenue long ago to be rid of the past. But the wave hath swallowed it—for ever, I would earnestly pray; and I am again free."

After these mysterious words, which left Grimes gaping with wonder, the stranger walked quickly away and was soon hidden behind a sand-hill.

Grimes and Dick then proceeded to their fishing. They had made one or two hauls with fair success, when the old man, who was busy with the tackling, saw something glittering amongst the fish in the net when he turned round after Dick had drawn it on board. It was a heavy casket, richly ornamented.

For years Grimes had dreamed of finding some rich and wonderful treasure; and now his dream had come true. The old man was nearly crazy with delight and excitement. Further fishing was abandoned, and all speed was made for the shore.

Grimes was so intent upon the casket that he did not notice Dick had slipped away, as soon as the boat had been anchored, in the direction taken by the stranger.

The weight of the casket showed Grimes that it contained a goodly store of money, or perhaps of jewels, and fearful of depreciating its value by breaking it open, he hid it in an oaken chest by his bedside, until he could get the tools necessary for picking the lock. That night a terrific storm raged upon the coast—a howling wind, thunder and lightning. Only then was it discovered that Dick was not in the house, that he had not yet returned from the shore. In the midst of the speculations as to his whereabouts, Grimes's wife, in a lull in the storm, heard whispering in the bedroom, where, unknown to her and Katherine, her husband had hidden the casket.

"Who is there in the chamber?" she asked him. "I hear it again."

"Hear! What?" Grimes replied gruffly.

"Something like an' it were a-whisperin' there," said his wife fearfully.

Grimes too thought he heard a whisper. The mysterious words of the stranger, "'Tis a doomed thing and accursed," came back to his memory, and trembling with superstitious fear he asked himself: Had the stranger spoken of the casket? Was this the doomed and accursed thing?

Katherine had no such fears. She too had heard the whispering, and went to the bedroom. Nobody was there. Then she opened the chest and saw the casket.

B B 2

"Why, father," she cried, running with it into the next room, "what a pretty fairing you have brought me! I'se warrant now you would not have told me on't till after the wakes, if I had not seen it."

Distracted by his superstitious fears, Grimes cried—

"Take it back—back, wench, into the chest again!" Then his miserliness overcoming his fear of the supernatural, he added roughly: "It was not for thee, hussey! A prize I picked up with the nets to-day."

The girl, in grave dismay, said that the casket must have come from some wreck. It was unholy spoil; she entreated her father to throw it back into the sea. But, however strong his superstitious fears might be, Grimes's avarice was stronger. He made no answer; and Katherine replaced the casket in the oak chest.

Mother and father and daughter sat in silence whilst the wind raged about the walls, and the thunder pealed, the lightning flashed, and the sea boomed in mighty waves upon the shore. Suddenly there came a lull in the storm, and in the intense stillness the sound of whispering was distinctly heard in the next room.

"Save us!" cried Mrs. Grimes in terror. "Save us! I hear it again!"

At that moment the door of the bedchamber burst open and the dumb servant walked into the room.

The only possible means of entrance into the bedchamber was through the door leading to the living-room, where the three were sitting, or through the bedroom window. How had Dick got into the bed-chamber?

"Plague take thee!" said Mrs. Grimes, "where hast thou been?"

"Where hast thou been, Dick?" her husband shouted.

For answer Dick pointed in the direction of the beach.

"How long hast thou been yonder? In the chamber, I mean," Grimes asked, anger and terror struggling for the mastery in his voice.

But "Dummy" made no sign. Vainly the three plied him with questions. The mother and father threatened, the daughter implored. Yet the man stood before them motionless, as if he heard nothing. Grimes's rage and terror was passing beyond control. He was about to strike the dumb man who had come so mysteriously from the bedchamber, when a strange light rising and falling upon the white-washed wall of the living-room attracted his attention. Rushing out into the yard he found the thatched roof of the barn on fire, caused in all probability by the lightning. The heavy rain prevented the flames from spreading, and Grimes, mounting upon the roof, was able to beat them out, despite the dense smoke.

But when he and his wife returned to the house both Dick and their daughter had disappeared. At first the old couple, although surprised, attached no particular importance to their absence, but as time passed and Katherine did not return they became anxious, and searched the farm, the sand-dunes and the beach. No sign or trace of her could they find.

For three days and nights they continued their fruitless search and inquiries, and at length could only come to the conclusion that their daughter had been taken away by Dick.

"Woe's me!" cried the weeping Mrs. Grimes. "My poor child! If I but knew what was come to her I think i' my heart I would be thankfu'. But what can have happen'd her? Unless it be Dick indeed, and yet I think the lad was honest, though lungeous at times and odd-tempered. By next market, surely, we shall ha' tidings fra' some end. But, I trow, 'tis that fearsome burden ye brought with you, George, fra' the sea that has been the cause of a' this trouble."

Grimes's wife put his own thoughts into words. Instantly he went to the bedchamber and took the casket from the chest. But now instead of being heavy it was light, as if it had been emptied of its contents, a change that added not a little to the old man's terror. Vowing the accursed thing should not did not remember that the box being empty would naturally float; he could only see a malign influence at work.

"It will haunt me as long as it is above ground," he thought, and, seizing the casket, carried it back to the farm. Arrived there, he set to work instantly to dig a deep hole in the peat-moss, and placing the casket at the bottom, covered it over and stamped the moss firmly down upon it. Nevertheless he had no peace.

THE LOST FARM

remain another night beneath his roof he threw it on to a turf-heap in the yard. On the following morning he took it far out to sea, but before casting it into the water regret at parting with such a treasure led him to examine it. To his surprise it was unlocked, and on lifting the lid he found the casket completely empty.

When the old fisherman had hauled his boat up on the beach, to his horror he saw the casket being rolled towards him by the incoming tide. He longed to flee, but fear held him fast to the spot where he stood. In his superstitious dread he "Noises horrid and unaccountable disturbed him," says Roby. "Demons had surely chosen his dwelling-place for their head-quarters. Nor day nor night could he rest—fancying that a whole legion of them were haunting him. He seemed to be the sport and prey of his own terrors; and with a heavy heart he resolved to quit, though suffering a grievous loss by the removal."

A few weeks later he removed to another small farm, but the story of the "haunted casket" had become known. The superstition and ignorance of the time added weird and creepy tales to those already spread by the terrified imaginings of Grimes and his wife. No other tenant could be found; no one would pass the house after dark; only the more venturous would pass it in the daytime. It was reputed to be the haunt of demons, and gradually the sand did its devastating work, and Grimes's old home became "The Lost Farm."

Still no word came of the missing Katherine, and day after day the old couple grew more sorrowful; the light had gone out of their home and existence. At last the husband, unable to bear the uncertainty, determined to set out in search of her. First he went to Churchtown. Some carts were drawn up before the inn door whilst their drivers refreshed themselves within, and hearing that they were on the way to Preston, Grimes, hoping he might find some trace of Katherine in that town—to which she had gone on various occasions—determined to avail himself of the carters' company on the road.

This was in 1746, a year after the Jacobite Rebellion, which brought ruin and death to many Lancashire gentlemen, as the previous rising had done in 1715. In Preston itself, in Manchester and Wigan, the heads of some of the executed rebels were stuck upon the town gateways, "to the great comfort of the loyal and well-disposed, and the grievous terror of the little children who passed in and out thereat." Some of the leaders escaped, and amongst them Charles Radcliffe, the titular Earl of Derwentwater,[1] who was supposed to have got aboard a ship for Scotland.

[1] Brother and heir of the Earl of Derwentwater, executed for his share in the 1715 Rebellion. The Derwentwater estates were confiscated to the Crown and the title forfeited, but Charles Radcliffe always called himself Earl of Derwentwater.

As old Grimes passed through the streets of Preston he met a large crowd of people accompanying a number of soldiers and constables, who were carefully guarding a prisoner in their midst. The prisoner's clothes were in rags; his haggard face bore signs of long watching and fatigue, but Grimes recognized him at once. It was his dumb servant Dick. Eager for news of Katherine he tried to get speech with the prisoner, but each time was roughly thrust back by the guards. Utterly bewildered and disconsolate, the old man sought lodgings at a humble inn. His appearance did not recommend him to the landlady, and but for the interposition of a well-dressed young man, who offered to pay for his bed and board, Grimes would have been bedless.

He had fallen into a troubled sleep when he was awakened by a caress and his daughter's voice, whispering, "Father, it is I!"

Before he could speak, she went on, "Hush! Be silent for your life and mine. You shall know all; but not now. Fear not for me, I'm safe; but I will not leave *him*—my companion—yonder unfortunate captive. Help me, and I'll contrive his rescue."

Grimes then made the discovery that Katherine was wearing men's clothes, and that it was she who had paid for his bed. But she could not give him the explanation he demanded. Time pressed, and he must wait to hear her story until the captive had been delivered.

"To-morrow night," she said, "bring your boat with four stout rowers to the quay at Preston Marsh. Let me see; ay, the moon is near two days old, and the tide will serve from nine till midnight. You know the channel well, and wait there until I come."

In the joy of seeing his daughter once

more Grimes gave the promise, and at earliest dawn was trudging back to Southport.

Whilst the fisherman was making his way homewards, an important interview was taking place between the Mayor of Preston and a stranger who had asked to see him on a matter of grave importance. The "matter" was the information that a plot had been laid for the escape of the prisoner, on his way to London. The mayor was greatly agitated, for the prisoner was the noted rebel, Charles Radcliffe, upon whose head a price had been set. His escape meant serious trouble for the mayor.

"If you be guided by me," suggested the stranger, "you may prevent this untoward event. Let him be conveyed with all speed aboard the King's ship that is in the Irish Channel yonder; so shall you quit your hands of him, and frustrate the plans of his confederates. This must be done secretly, or his friends may get knowledge of the matter, who have had a ship long waiting for him privily on the coast to convey him forthwith to Scotland."

Charles Radcliffe was imprisoned at the Bull Inn, and thither the town clerk and the stranger, who had seemingly betrayed him, were soon hurrying.

"We come, sir, to announce your removal," said the clerk. "But first we search for plots. This rebel's disguise—where sayest thou, it is concealed?"

"Upon his person," answered the betrayer. Radcliffe was forced to take off his clothes, and underneath them was seen a woman's dress—the one worn by Katherine Grimes at the time of her disappearance from the farm. Overcome with surprise and emotion at the betrayal of his secret plans, he was removed from the inn to the town gaol for safe keeping.

An hour before midnight Radcliffe was driven in a closed carriage, his arms and his legs in chains, to the quay at Preston Marsh, in company with the mayor and the town-clerk. Alongside a wooden pier lay a fishing-boat in which were five men, four at the oars and one at the helm. Radcliffe was lifted into the boat, being followed by the gaoler, whose duty it was to hand him over to the captain of the King's cutter, with some of his attendants. The mayor and the town-clerk, satisfied that they had seen their prisoner in safe custody, remained upon the pier, until the little vessel disappeared in the darkness. After nearly four hours, as they passed the lights of Lytham, and came near the open sea, the stranger, who had betrayed Lord Derwentwater, came out of the cabin where he had been sleeping. A light was hoisted to the mainmast, and in a few moments there came an answering flash from some little distance away: a little while longer, and in the faint light of the dawn they saw a ship approaching them. In a few moments she was alongside.

After some delay and with much difficulty the prisoner was transferred from the boat to the vessel by the gaoler and his assistants. But instead of a smart and clean man-of-war they found themselves upon the deck of a trading vessel in which the smells of tar, fish and grease struggled for the mastery.

"So, master," cried the captain. "We had nigh slipped hawser and away. Why, here have we been beating about and about for three long nights; by day we durst not be seen inshore. Yon cruiser overhauls everything from a crab to a crab-louse. What! got part of your company in the gyves! Where is the Earl?"

The gaoler began to suspect that all was not as it should be.

"Hold!" he said to the captain.

"The vessel goes not on her voyage until I and two of my friends here depart with the boat; we go not farther with our prisoner. The remaining two will suffice to see him delivered at headquarters." Then, his suspicions increasing, he added, "I have a warrant to commit the rebel unto the safe keeping of—ay the captain of His Majesty's cutter, the *Dart*. But this is as frowsy and fusty a piece of ship's-timber as ever stowed coals and cod's tails between her hatches."

No one in the little band was more surprised than Charles Radcliffe. He had looked upon his fate as sealed after his betrayal. But now the stranger came forward, and speaking directly to Radcliffe, said: "My lord, I am no traitor, though until now labouring under the imputation; but you are amongst friends. Thanks to a woman's wits, we are, despite guards, bolts and fetters, aboard the vessel which was waiting for us when you were surprised and seized, unfortunately, as we were trying to make our escape towards the coast. With the aid of my parent, I have been at last successful. You are now free."

The stranger, and supposed betrayer, was none other than Katherine, disguised in male attire and speaking in a "muffled" voice!

Probability must not be sought for in old legends, and we must accept the story as it has come down to us from the romantic pen of Roby. The moment Katherine spoke in her natural voice Charles Radcliffe recognized her. She then said to the captain—

"Captain, we have nabbed as cunning a gaoler as ever took rogue to board in a stone crib. We will trouble thee to use thy craft; undo these fetters, prithee!"

The unfortunate gaoler, who found himself a prisoner, carried out her bidding.

"He must with you, captain," continued the intrepid Katherine when Rad-cliffe was freed from his irons, "till you can safely leave him and his companions ashore; but use him well for his vocation's sake. My lord," she said, turning to Radcliffe, "through weal and woe I have been your counsellor—your friend; but we must now part—'tis fitting we should. While you were in jeopardy that alone could excuse my flight. Should better times come——"

Then the brave girl broke down, and taking farewell of Radcliffe, hurried with her father to the boat. As they left the vessel's side old Grimes saw the stranger who, as he believed, had cast the haunted casket into the sea. There is little doubt but that the casket, filled with money, was placed in Grimes's boat in order to help Radcliffe, who had posed for a year as a dumb servant, to escape to the ship upon which, owing to Katherine's astuteness he now found himself. The old fisherman saw only a supernatural agency in the whole affair of the casket; his weakness and superstition had been cleverly played upon both by Radcliffe and the stranger in order to facilitate the former's escape.

The story of "The Lost Farm," however, did not have a happy ending.

When the gaoler and his assistants did not return to Preston, inquiries were made which showed that the titular Earl of Derwentwater had not been taken to the King's cutter. The trading-vessel, with Radcliffe and the gaoler on board, was hurrying under all the sail it could muster, to Scotland. But it had no chance against the superior fleetness of the King's cutter, which speedily overtook it. Once more Charles Radcliffe became a prisoner, and being carried to London was there executed as a traitor. With him ended one of the many families of Radcliffes which sprang originally from Radcliffe Tower.

LIVERPOOL AND LIGHTHOUSES

IT is difficult to believe that our ancestors were so strongly opposed to the erection of lighthouses that, notwithstanding the dangerous nature of the coast, it was not until 1762 that the merchants of Liverpool were sufficiently alive to their own interests, to promote an Act of Parliament under which the lighthouses on the Cheshire coast were erected. A hundred years previously a Mr. Reading—five years after the first lighthouse in England was erected at Plymouth in 1665,—had applied for a patent to empower him to erect lighthouses along the western coast of England. At that time every proposal was made the subject of royal grants and monopolies, the Sovereign giving the individual the right by a document which was called a patent. This system of the granting of monopolies was one of the most iniquitous of the many unjust powers then held by the Crown. Court favourites were bribed by monopoly seekers to push their claims with the monarch, who, and especially in the case of the Stuarts, not infrequently granted a monopoly in return for a large sum of money paid to himself. The monopoly holders naturally looked to recoup themselves from their charges to the public for the monopoly, whatever it might be. Thus Mr. Reading, if the patent for these lighthouses had been given to him, would have had the right to levy a toll for their maintenance. The Mayor and Corporation of Liverpool were strenuously opposed to the erection of any lighthouses on the coast, and sent the following letter to Sir Gilbert Ireland, who then represented the city in Parliament—

"SIR :—Yesterday we received a copie of the Ord^r enclosed, wherein you will understand what day the Committee for Grievances will meet to Consider of Reading's Patent for Light Houses.

Therefore wee make it our humble request to you, that on behalf of this Burrough you will be pleased to appeare on Parliam^t at or before that tyme. In regard those light houses will be no benefit to our Mariners, but a hurt, and Expose them to more danger, if trust to them and also be a very great and unnecessary burden and charge to them. Wee are S^r

"Your most humble servants
"THOMAS JOHNSON (Mayor).
"THOMAS AYNDOC (Mayor in 1655).
"HENRY CORLESS (Mayor in 1661).
"JOHN STURZAKER.
"THOMAS BICKERSTETH (Mayor in 1669)."

"*Liverpoole, 5th Jan.* 1670."

A petition seems to have been presented to Parliament to protest against Reading's scheme, for the Order of Parliament enclosed in the letter from the Corporation to Sir Gilbert Ireland, was as follows. It will be observed that the date written in Latin, "Lune," standing for Monday—

"*Lune* 19° *die Decembris* 1670.
"Ordered—That the Committee of Grievances does sitt upon Wednesday moneth next, and doe examine the matter of Grievance formerly Complayned of against Mr. Reading and others by petition referred to the said Committee. And that Mr. Reading does cause notice to be sent to the Parties concerned.
"WILLIAM GOLDSBOROUGH,
"Cler. Dom. Com."

"This is a true Coppy of y^e oridginall order."

No more was heard of this scheme, it would therefore appear that Liverpool's opposition to it, through Sir Gilbert Ireland, was successful.

LIVERPOOL'S OLD TOWER

LIVERPOOL, EARLY IN THE SEVENTEENTH CENTURY, SHOWING THE TOWER

FOR five hundred years The Tower at Liverpool was closely connected with the fortunes both of the place and of the great Stanley family.

Some time in the fourteenth century the site between the Exchange and George's Dock, near the bottom of Water Street, upon which until 1819, there stood a pile of mediæval buildings known as The Tower, came into the possession of the Lathoms of Lathom House, Lords of Knowsley and many other manors roundabout.

In the reign of Edward III. the head of the family was Sir Thomas Lathom, an old man, whose only daughter Isabel was his heiress. John Stanley, the founder of the house of Derby, was the second son of Sir William Stanley of Hooton, and as such had to make his fortune with his sword. At a tournament held at Winchester towards the close of Edward III.'s reign the young Lancastrian esquire distinguished himself so greatly by his prowess that he was knighted on the spot; but, what was even more satis-factory, his prowess and good looks conquered the heart of the Lady Isabel of Lathom, who was present at the tournament with her father. They were married shortly afterwards, and among the many gifts of land from his father-in-law, Sir John Stanley, received the site of The Tower. In all probability there was a house standing there at the time, for after Sir John had been rewarded with the lordship of the Isle of Man for his gallantry in the Irish wars, he was given permission by Henry IV. to "fortify, embattle, and crenellate" his house by the river-side at Liverpool. For close upon four centuries The Tower was the seaside residence of the Derby family and the place of their embarkation for the Isle of Man, where they kept regal state. They had their own vessels, and Lord Stanley in the old ballad of "Lady Bessie," tells Elizabeth of York, "the White Rose of England," that he will undertake to send her messenger, Humphrey Brereton, across the sea to her future husband, Henry VII.

27

Derby passed to the Stanleys of Bickerstaffe. The interest in Liverpool, the pride in filling its municipal offices and giving the people hospitality at The Tower, had been a tradition for more than three hundred years with the Lathom Stanleys. It did not exist amongst the Bickerstaffe Stanleys, and within two years of Earl James's death, The Tower was sold to the Clayton family, and being let to the corporation was made into the borough gaol ; and its chapel was converted into Assembly Rooms !

Some ᶦforty years later the Liverpool Corporation purchased The Tower for £1535 10s. ; and although the New Borough Gaol was built in 1786, the old home of the Earls of Derby was occupied by debtors and felons until July 1811. During the next eight years it stood empty, then it was pulled down and the materials sold by auction. They fetched two hundred pounds, a corn-miller called Barrow being the purchaser. With the material he built a steam corn-mill in Chaucer Street, Scotland Road, which he called the Castle Mills. A few years later these mills were burnt to the ground, and for long afterwards the charred ruins remained untouched. Then they were carted away as rubbish, and a brewery was built upon the site.

Thus every trace of the old Tower was swept away. Save for the old chronicles and the old print reproduced in the illustration, it might never have existed. Yet there is a record—the courtesy of Commerce to History.

The site was sold to a great firm of ironmasters, Bailey Brothers of South Wales, who built warehouses upon it. In 1856 the alignment of Water Street, under the municipal improvements, was set back ; the warehouses were pulled down, and a great pile of offices, called Tower Buildings, was built. On the south side of the inner quadrangle of these buildings a tablet was placed upon the wall, with this inscription—

Has Aedes
Situm olim castelli
Comitum de Derby
Denuo construxit
Negotiis pacisque artibus fovendis
Dedicavit
Jos. Bailey, Eq. Aur.
Anno salutis MDCCCLVII.
Architectus—J. A. Picton.

Which, being freely translated, runs—

" Joseph Bailey Esquire on this site, formerly that of the castle of the Earls of Derby, has erected this building for the prosecution of the labours of Art and Peace. In the year of our Salvation 1857. Architect, J. A. Picton."

Although the Tower of Liverpool was not rented by the Corporation for a gaol until 1737, there is ample proof that some portion of it had been used as a town prison during its occupancy by the earls of Derby. In a rare book, published in 1691, entitled *The Cry of the Oppressed Poor Debtors in England*, it is called the *Gaol of Liverpool*. The following letter speaks for itself. It was given " under the hand and seal " of its unfortunate writer on November 7, 1690—

" From the Gaol of Liverpoole
in Lancashire.
" Sir,
" Thomas Morgan of Liverpoole, chyrurgeon, having a wife and five children, falling lame, for which reason he was not able to follow his practice ; his wife also at the same time falling sick of a fever, and her children visited with the small-pox ; fell to decay and was cast into the prison of Liverpoole for about £11 of debt ; the said prison being about 16 foot in length and

12 foot in breadth, in which was two houses of office it being but one room, and no yard to walk in. In which prison the said Mr. Morgan was locked up a year and a quarter, in all which time neither he nor any of the other barous usage of the said Mr. Morgan, his wife making complaint and seeking redress, she also was sent to prison and shut up close prisoner in another room, and not suffered to come to her husband, she having at the same time a child of

THE TOWER IN THE EIGHTEENTH CENTURY

prisoners had any bedding, or straw to lodge on, nor any allowance of meat or drink, so that the said Mr. Morgan was necessitated to catch mice with a trap to eat, for to keep himself from starving; and also felons and highwaymen were put into the same prison with the debtors; of which hard and bar- three months old 'sucking at her breast without any allowance for her maintenance but what she had out of charity from her neighbours.' Of all which barbarities the said Mr. Morgan complaining, instead of redress, the gaoler, Thomas Row, beat the said Mr. Morgan and put him in irons."

F F 2

MARY MELVIN OF THE MERSEY SIDE

THIS was once a favourite song in Liverpool and the neighbourhood, and is found in many of the old "broadsides" which were so popular before the days of cheap newspapers.

GIVE ear with patience to my relation,
  All you that ever felt Cupid's dart,
I'm captivated and ruinated,
  By a young female that made me smart.
My mind's tormented, I can't prevent it,
  Her glancing beauty has me destroy'd,
I speak sincerely, I suffered dearly—
  For Mary Melvin of the Mersey side.

In the month of May when the lambkins play,
  By the river-side as I chanc'd to rove,
There I spied Mary, both bright and airy,
  And singing sweetly as she did rove.
I got enchanted, I throbbed and panted,
  Like one delirious I stood and cried,
"Ah! lovely creature, the boast of nature,
  Did Cupid send you to the Mersey side?"

She made this answer, "It's all romancing
  For you to flatter a single dame;
I'm not so stupid, or dup'd by Cupid,
  So I defy you on me to scheme;
My habitation is near this plantation,
  I feed my flock by the river-side;
Therefore don't tease me, and you will please me,"
  Said Mary Melvin of the Mersey side.

I said, "My charmer, my soul's alarmer,
  Your glancing beauty did me ensnare;
If I've offended, I never intended
  To hurt your feelings, I do declare.
You sang so sweetly, and so discreetly,
  You cheer'd the woods and valleys wide,
That fam'd Apollo your voice would follow,
  Should he but hear you near the Mersey side."

"Young man, you're dreaming, or you are scheming,
  You're like the serpent that tempted Eve,
Your wily speeches do sting like leeches,
  But all your flattery shan't me deceive.
Your vain delusion is an intrusion;
  For your misconduct I must you chide;
Therefore retire, it is my desire,"
  Said Mary Melvin of the Mersey side.

"Don't be so cruel, my dearest jewel,
  I'm captivated, I really vow;
To show I'm loyal, make no denial,
  Here is my hand, and I'll wed you now.
I want no sporting, nor tedious courting,
  But instantly I'll make you my bride;
Therefore surrender, I'm no pretender,
  Sweet Mary Melvin of the Mersey side."

She then consented, and quite contented
  Unto the church we went straightway,
And quickly hurried, and both got married,
  And joined our hearts on that very day.
Her parents bless'd us, and then caress'd us;
  A handsome portion they did provide;
We bless the day that we chanc'd to stray
  By the lovely banks on the Mersey side.

THE DRIVER OF THE FIRST PASSENGER TRAIN

THE driver of the first passenger train in England was a youth called Edward Entwistle, who was born at Tyldesley Banks, near Wigan, in 1815. At the age of eleven he was made an apprentice in the large machine shops belonging to the Bridgewater Trust in Manchester, his parents having decided that he should be an engineer. It was in these works that the "Rocket," the first passenger locomotive, was built under the direction and according to the plans of its inventor, George Stephenson. Young Entwistle took the keenest interest in the progress of the engine. When the Liverpool and

Manchester Railway was finished and the "Rocket" completed, Stephenson looked about for a driver. The foreman of the shops was consulted, but after a day or two reported that he had no man he could suggest, but that if the great inventor would take the young apprentice Entwistle, he could recommend him highly. The steward of the Trust, therefore, was applied to and readily gave a written permission for the youth to go with Stephenson. Entwistle, however, was only informed of his new labours after all the arrangements had been made; but he seized the opportunity gladly, and set to work to make himself thoroughly acquainted with the new engine. He was then only fifteen.

The opening of the new railway, which attracted the attention of the whole country, was fixed for Monday, September 15, 1830. On Sunday, Stephenson and young Entwistle took the "Rocket" for a trial trip, running over about one-half of the track. The following day both were on the engine which made that historic journey from Liverpool to Manchester, drawing behind it some of the most distinguished people in the land, a journey whose triumph was marred by the tragic accident to Mr. Huskisson.[1] During the return journey from Manchester the young apprentice's hand was on the throttle.

When the line was opened for general traffic Entwistle was given sole charge of the "Rocket," and for two years made two round trips every day between Liverpool and Manchester, one in the morning and the other in the afternoon. But the work was a serious strain on a youth; he became ill and found he was losing his nerve. He, therefore, asked to be relieved of his charge, and was told by Stephenson that he was only an apprentice and

[1] See "The Liverpool and Manchester Railway."

would have to stay where he was. To this Entwistle replied that he had not been apprenticed to a locomotive. Stephenson admitted the point, and through his kindness Entwistle secured a place as second engineer on one of the coasting steamers belonging to the Bridgewater Trust, on which he completed his seven years' apprenticeship, and remained a year afterwards.

When he was twenty-two Entwistle emigrated to America, but on landing in New York he found times were so bad, business stagnant, and money so scarce, that he could only earn a dollar a day as an engineer on a steamer called the *Troy*, which ran in the Hudson River and Long Island Sound. He was a man of much resource and ingenuity, for when the *Troy* was condemned he took her engines and set them up in a rolling-mill on shore.

In 1844 he migrated to Chicago, and for some twelve years was in charge of stationary engines in that place, with the exception of one summer, when he and a man called Perrier ran the *Rossite*, which was one of the first steamers worked by propellers on the lakes. During the next thirty-three years Entwistle had charge of the engines of two great mills in the State of Iowa; at one of these, the Ankery Mills, he remained for twenty-one years. When he was seventy-four Entwistle retired to a farm he had purchased forty years before, and at the age of eighty-one it was recorded of him that he had personally superintended the construction of a new barn, helping in the work himself. He was said to be energetic, quick of speech and motion, and possessed of very decided opinions, but his greatest pride—and a just pride—was in having been the first man to drive a passenger engine, and so inaugurate a method of locomotion which revolutionised the world.

LIVERPOOL *VERSUS* LONDON

IT is very seldom that one town brings an action in a court of law against another, but in 1799, Liverpool brought an action in the Court of the Exchequer against the City of London. The question between the rising seaport and the metropolis arose out of the exemption from the town dues, payable in Liverpool, on ships and goods belonging to the citizens of London. By the terms of many royal charters granted to the capital, the citizens and freemen were exempted from paying local tolls in any part of the country, this right overriding any local bye-laws, or charters given to other cities and towns. As early as 1695, this right of the Londoners began to be a serious matter to the finances of Liverpool, and when the cheesemongers of London resisted payment in that year an action was brought in which the rights of the Londoners were upheld. During the next hundred years the customs of Liverpool increased by leaps and bounds, and this exemption therefore became a valuable privilege.

But it was discovered that not only were London merchants benefiting considerably by their right, but that Liverpool merchants, by an ingenious device, were doing the same. Up to 1777, the freedom of the City of London could be purchased for what was called a fine, so all a Liverpool merchant had to do was to pay the fine and, hey presto ! he became a citizen of London with a right to bring all his goods into Liverpool free of toll or due.

When the freedom of the City of London by purchase was abolished, many Liverpool merchants found a considerable difference in their incomes, but there was still another means of claiming the right of Londoners. For the sum of forty or fifty pounds they could be elected to some one of the smaller Companies of the City of London, thus obtaining the freedom, and by this small payment enjoyed the privilege of putting many hundreds of pounds in their own pockets, which by right should have gone to the Liverpool Corporation. But there were occasions when these gentlemen were caught in their own trap. Freemen of the City of London elected to one of the Companies are liable to be nominated as sheriff to the City, and pay a fine of five hundred pounds if they decline to serve. It is on record that more than one Liverpool merchant was so elected, and as it was impossible for them to carry out the duties, they were obliged to pay the fine. Once a Liverpool merchant, named Leigh, actually served as Sheriff of London.

By the year 1799 the situation had become intolerable ; week by week more vessels came to Liverpool, more merchandise crowded her warehouses and quays, and yet the increasing number of ships and the increasing amount of merchandise was obliged to be passed free of all tolls and duties, because of the rights of the " freed men of London." The Corporation therefore determined to bring the matter to an issue, and practically got a verdict in their favour, for at the trial held in London in April 1799, the jury decided that the citizens of London were entitled to the exemption for their goods and wares given them by the charter, but that such exemption belonged exclusively to those who were resident freemen within the liberties of London.

This verdict put an end to what was in reality a system of robbery of Liverpool by her own children, for it was scarcely worth while for any merchant to have a house in London and keep up an establishment there merely in order to avoid the payment of the town dues and dock tolls of Liverpool.

THE RECTOR OF PRESCOT'S HORSE=SHOE

A HORSE-SHOE, always supposed to be the emblem of good luck, lost the Rector of Prescot both his tithes and his position, in the reign of James I. During his progress through Lancashire, after his famous visit to Hoghton Tower, James stayed with the Earl of Derby at Lathom House. Whilst riding alone through a country lane, he saw something lying in one of the ruts, which, by its glittering, attracted his

He therefore commanded that the great tithes of Prescot should henceforward be paid to King's College, Cambridge, and the Rector to be reduced to the rank of a Vicar.

Writing of Prescot, some curious illustrations of the government of a manor in the old days are given in a book entitled, "An Abstract of the Proceedings in Prescot Court, commencing anno 1509, and ending 1716." The town was governed by four

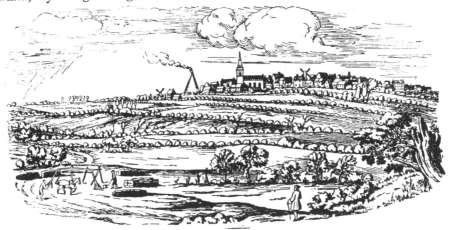

PRESCOT IN THE EIGHTEENTH CENTURY

attention. The King therefore got down from his horse, and finding the glittering object to be a silver horse-shoe, he put it in his pocket, thinking it belonged either to his host or to one of the many noblemen in his train. After dinner King James produced the horse-shoe and inquired who was the owner. To his intense and undisguised astonishment it was claimed by the Rector of Prescot, who was present.

" Well," said the King, " if the produce of your rectory is such as to enable you to shoe your horse with silver, it is time that money so wasted was appropriated for better purposes."

men, who were called, " The Four Men," and their government appears to have been not only paternal, but not a little tyrannical. These are some of the entries.

" *1534.* Ordered that every man that assaulteth another shall forfeit 3s. 4d., and if blood be drawn, 6s. 8d. more. *1536.* That the inhabitants make their middensteads by the direction of the four men of the town. *1541.* That no person be permitted to inhabit the town without the copyholders' consent, and to bring six sureties. *1542.* That ale shall be sold at two pence per gallon the best, and three halfpence per gallon for the second sort. *1554.* Cicely Hitchmough, formerly pre-

-H

sented to be a woman of evil carriage, and to be expelled the town, referred to my Lord to be punished. *1565.* Orders for several to leave the town who have abused their neighbours. *1566.* That George Saddler is a common drunkard. That the wife of George Saddler is a thief or petty filcher. *1570.* An order that young fellows who fight, and who have no money to pay their amercements, shall sit in the stocks three days and three nights ; and if any relieve them to sit in the stocks in their room. *1583.* Catharine Dempster banished the town, being of evil government. *1599.* Ordered that no person shall fell or carry away any timber or poles out of Prescot Wood, without the consent of the four men on pain of 6*s.* 8*d.*"

Any vestige of such a wood disappeared long ago, but there were some fields to the west of the town known as " The Wood," and it is conjectured this was the site of Prescot Wood. " *1607.* An order against putting butter on bread or cakes on forfeiture of five shillings per time. An order for ale to be sold at one penny per quart out of doors. *1609.* An order

that the constables pump on Alice Allerton, *alias* Miller, so often as she comes into the streets to chide or abase herself. *1613.* Mr. Walban presented for felling eighty trees in Prescot Wood, fined 2*s.* a piece, £8. *1621.* A large presentment made by the four men concerning several abuses in the wood. *1630.* Richard Halsall presented for saying the town was governed by fools, 3*s.* 4*d.* Item, saying he would fell timber in spite of all the town, 3*s.* 4*d.* *1633.* An order for banishing out of the town a woman called Pretty Peggy. *1672.* Several presented for bringing corn to market better at the top of the sack than at the bottom. *1683.* One presented for baking bread without licence. *1696.* Mr. Parr, for tussling with Esq Cross, and Esq Cross for tussling with him again."

The last entry is dated 1716, with a memorandum appended, " And here the Abstract Book breaks off and takes no further notice of any presentments, orders, etc."

The question of cutting wood seems to have been a sore point with the townsfolk.

A PRODIGIOUS APPETITE

DURING the long war with France at the close of the eighteenth century a new gaol built at Liverpool, in 1786, was used for nearly twenty years afterwards as a depôt for French prisoners of war. One of these men, a Pole by birth, but who had fought in the service of France, excited the astonishment of the whole town by his prodigious appetite. The man's name was Charles Domery. Nothing came amiss to his insatiable appetite— dogs, rats, cats and candles. Raw meat was his favourite delicacy. Dr. Cochrane,

a Liverpool physician, was deeply interested in Domery, as a " case," and on one occasion, wishing to test his powers, invited some friends to see him make a meal. In their presence it is recorded that Domery ate fourteen pounds of raw meat and two pounds of candles and drank five bottles of porter. This mighty eater is described as being pleasant in manner, obliging and inoffensive. He was six feet two inches in height and although well proportioned was rather thin. His voracity was doubtless caused by disease.

LIVERPOOL'S FIRST THEATRE

THE first theatre in Liverpool was built in 1745 in the Old Ropery, opposite the end of Drury Lane, by Alderman Thomas Steers. But as it was only fifty feet by twenty feet it speedily became too small for the growing dramatic requirements of the town, and four years later a second theatre, a plain, neat brick building with a frontage of twenty-seven yards and a depth of sixteen yards, equipped with boxes, pit, and gallery, was opened. It stood near the old theatre at the corner of two streets, and a new street immediately fronting it was called Drury Lane after the famous street in London. Its rent was sixty-five pounds a year, its current expenses were ten pounds a night, and the highest receipts on a single night were ninety-two pounds.

For some years Messrs. Gibson and Ridout were the joint managers and principal actors. Of their popularity, and the estimation in which they were held at Liverpool, the following anecdote is told: "At the time when Garrick was at the zenith of his popularity, two of the dramatic connoisseurs of Liverpool having to visit London, were requested to attend Drury Lane and report on the performance of the celebrated actor. They did so, and on their return in answer to questions, they reported that ' Garrick was all very well, but he was nothing to Gibson and Ridout!'"

Liverpool theatre-goers in those days had a long and varied entertainment for their money. Seats in the boxes were three shillings each, the pit was two shillings, and the gallery was one shilling. The doors opened at five o'clock, the performance beginning at seven. On Monday, August 8, 1768, this was the programme presented: " By Comedians from the Theatres Royal in London." First there came *Othello*, at the end of the second act of which " A New Scotch Dance called 'The Highland Reel' was danced by Mr. Fishar, Mrs. Manesiere, and Miss Besford, apprentice to Mr. Fishar." After the curtain had fallen on the dead bodies of Desdemona and Othello there came " A New Pantomime Dance call'd 'The Village Romps,'" and to conclude the evening's bill, a farce— *High Life Below Stairs*. One of the rules of the theatre was: ' Not any money under the Full Price to be taken during the whole Performance nor any servants admitted to the Gallery without paying " ; and another, " No person whatever can be admitted behind the scenes." This theatre had a successful career for about twenty-three years, and then, a new one having been built in Williamson Square, it gradually fell into disuse, and ultimately became a carrier's warehouse and shed for the fire-engine. It disappeared under one of the earliest of Liverpool's Improvement Acts, and its site is now supposed to be covered by Brunswick Street.

THE BUILDING OF A LIVERPOOL STREET

CURIOUS and interesting little histories, which throw a vivid light on the past, are sometimes hidden in the names of streets. Fenwick Street in Liverpool is an example. The land on which it was built in the reign of Charles II., belonged to Sir Edward Moore, who had married Dorothy, the daughter of Sir Richard Fenwick of Meldon. The Moore family had been staunch Parliamentarians, and Sir Edward's father, Colonel John Moore, had been one of the regicides who had judged King Charles I. and condemned him to death. For this the whole of his estates —and he owned considerable property in and about Liverpool—were confiscated to the Crown at the restoration of Charles II., and his son was reduced to beggary. But Sir Edward was fortunate in his choice of a wife, as is shown by the " instructions to his son," in which he gives four reasons for naming the new street Fenwick Street.

The first in importance apparently was that she was the daughter of Sir William Fenwick ; the second was that with her fortune he had " disengaged ten thousand pounds principal money of a debt contracted by his unfortunate father " ; the third that the Moore estates having been confiscated at the Restoration, his wife had petitioned the House of Lords for a reversal, and that owing to her influence and activity, " the King was graciously pleased, in consideration of her father's merits and her own sufferings, to grant John Moore's whole estate to such feoffers in trust, as she, Dorothy Moore, daughter and co-heir of Sir William Fenwick, should name," which was tantamount to restoring the estates to the regicide's son. The fourth reason was " that to add to all these mercies, which God was pleased to make her an instrument in, to sweeten them the more to us, He hath been pleased to bless me with four sons and two daughters."

A small street near the southern end of Fenwick Street was called the Old Ropery, and is the record of a type of obstinacy which, some two hundred years later, special legislation was required to overcome, in the shape of an Act of Parliament making the selling of property for public improvements compulsory. But when Sir Edward Moore built Fenwick Street, William Bushell, a rope-maker, was able to openly defy him. This Bushell had a house in Castle Street with a long field behind it, and in the field he had made a ropewalk. When Fenwick Street was laid out, this ropewalk made a barrier right across it, and although Bushell was offered as much as thirty pounds for a piece of ground ten yards wide, he resolutely refused to sell, or to remove his ropewalk elsewhere. Sir Edward got over the difficulty by building a bridge over the obdurate Bushell's property, which was called the Dry Bridge. In 1802 this bridge was still in existence, as is shown in a record of an exchange of property between the Liverpool Corporation and the Trustees of the Blue School, in which are mentioned " A dwelling house at the east end of Dry Bridge," " The Ropewalk under the Dry Bridge," and " A cellar in Dry Bridge."

Between Fenwick Street and Castle Street there were a number of narrow alleys, one of which was named " Bridges Alley " by Sir Edward Moore in a moment of unusual humour, for he was a stern Puritan and a hard landlord. " The reason why I named it Bridges Alley," he says, " was because it lay betwixt two bridges, the one at the west end, where never water runs under, made for to spin under ; the other at the east end is my tenant, Thomas Bridge ; a drunken fellow ; upon which these verses were made as follows :—

" ' In old, bridges for water were,
But these are made for other fare ;
The one for spinning, and, it's said,
The other's for the drunken trade.
Let this be set to England's wonder ;
Two bridges, and no water under ! ' "

OLD STREETS AND BUILDINGS OF LIVERPOOL

OLD PIER HEAD, LIVERPOOL

THE Liverpool to which King John granted a charter in 1207, consisted of the Castle and a few streets of wattle and clay houses. The Castle commanded the slope to the beach on three sides; on the fourth or north side a street ran from the Castle gate. There were only two approaches to the town from the land side, one from the east, which, crossing the Pool brook approached the sea by way of Water Street; the other from the north, curving westward, formed the line of Tithebarn Street and Chapel Street. Between these two streets ran the High Street, or, as it was called then, Joggler or Jugloure Street. And at each intersection stood a cross, one called the White Cross and the other the High Cross. This was originally the main street of the town.

It is first mentioned in the reign of Henry V. in a deed in which Henry de Bretherton conveyed to Hugh de Botyl a parcel of ground in a garden in "Juglour Streete." Again in the reign of Henry VI. there is a conveyance between the same parties of two houses at the "Corner near the High Cross." Liverpool's first Town Hall stood in the High Street, being called, before the Reformation, St. Mary's Hall. It seems to have been a thatched building, as there is an order in the town records for its being covered with slates for the first time in 1567. Not only was it a Town Hall, it was likewise a Custom House, a lock-up for prisoners, a Mansion House—the Mayor being required to keep the glass in repair at his own expense—and also a banqueting house.

In the time of Queen Elizabeth the Town Hall was apparently lent for private entertainments, by the Mayor and Corporation, for in 1571 we find this order of the Council:—

"We find necessarie for the upholdyng better and long continewyng of owre comyn hall of this town in good order of reparacion of the same, that noe licence be or shall be grauntyd and givyn to make any wedding diners or playes of dawnsying therein to the damagying, decayng, or falling of the floore of the same, and if it chaunce upon any urgent cause, or earnest re- is of necessitie used as a prison house for the receipt of all persons here committed for or by reason of anie cryme or debte, which is not a fitte place for yt purpose, and therefore it was moved by Mr. Maior that some other place might be provided and appointed for a common gaole, where- unto Alaien Gayney made answer and proffered unto Mr. Maior and the towne,

HIGH STREET

quest not deniable, any licence to be givyn therein, that thereby the same licence the partie or parties soe obteyn- ing licence shall pay to the comyn cooffer for everie such licence fyve shilling, usuel money."

Eight 'years later the Mayor seems to have been incommoded by the presence of prisoners kept in the Town Hall, for the Council in that year decided :—" Foras- much as yt is considered that great incon- venience doe in sundriewise growe, that hitherto this comyn haule hath bene and a certain house by him latelie builded near unto the sea syde."

The line of buildings in the High Street seems to have been irregular, for in his *Rental*, Edward Moore, speaking of a house occupied by Alderman Peter Lurt- ing, who was Mayor in 1663, says there was " a stately room betwixt the house and the street to build on." From the same source we learn that there were small shops as well as good houses in the old High Street—" Query, how the town came by the little shops where the women now sell apples and the cobbler works ?

Because, in an exchange from Sir Richard Mullineux, I find them granted to my grandfather, John Moore."

This is a question that must remain unanswered for ever.

All that was left of the High Street was removed in 1856, the London and Liverpool Chambers being built upon its site.

There used to stand in Dale Street, at the corner of Hale Street, an old inn which, although called the " Hammer and Anvil," was always known as " The Mayor's House," from the fact that in some long ago time it had been the residence of a Mayor of Liverpool. He was said to have paved the street in front of the house with his own hands. When George Fox, the founder of the Quakers, went to Liverpool in 1669, he recorded in his diary, " We landed at Liverpool and went to the mayor's house, it being an inn." This has always been considered a mistake on Fox's part, as in that year the chief magistrate was William, Lord Strange, during the earlier part, and he was followed in the later part by Thomas Bickersteth, a very wealthy merchant. As neither of these gentlemen would be likely to keep an inn, Fox has been accused of a deliberate misstatement. It has also been supposed that the Sunday dinners given by the Mayor took place at the Mayor's House—because of its name. But they were held at the Town Hall. These Sunday dinners continued for a long time. One of the ministers in the town was always invited, with about half a dozen other guests. At the start they were very frugal repasts, consisting of a single joint and a pudding. If wine was given it was removed after each guest's glass had been filled. But gradually the meals became more and more elaborate and grew into so great a strain upon the mayor's resources that they were ultimately abandoned. In 1721, the then Mayor died insolvent, and his bills for entertaining not having been paid, they were honourably discharged by the Corporation, but at the same time it was decided that in future no Mayor should

THE MAYOR'S HOUSE

THE OLD CORN EXCHANGE

receive his stipend until the end of his year of office, nor until all his entertainment bills had been met.

The Town Hall served many purposes, as we have seen; it was also used as an Exchange, the open space in front of it being allotted to the buyers and sellers of corn, it then being the custom for the corn trade to be carried on in the open air. This space is given in old maps as the " Corn Market." But when the merchants of Liverpool found it necessary to erect a special building for their cotton and other transactions in 1803, those in the corn trade thought the time had come to provide a separate Exchange for themselves. This was done in 1807, when a Corn Exchange was built upon the south side of Brunswick Street at a cost of ten thousand pounds, the money being raised by shares of one hundred pounds each. There were many in the trade who opposed the plan, preferring the old primitive system of open-air sales and the old methods, to the centralisation of buying and selling

under one roof. This preference continued after the opening of the Corn Exchange, for two years later we find Troughton writing thus in defence of the plan :—" Ancient systems, established customs, and immediate profit, are remarkably venerable in the eyes of some ; but when the great increase of the corn trade, the portion of time and labour which are consumed in visiting the different warehouses for the purposes of buying and selling, and the enormous expense of travelling, which it is intended to obviate, are considered, it will perhaps be pronounced by those who are guided by their understandings more than by their prejudices, an excellent expedient."

During the next forty years the Liverpool corn trade increased so rapidly that several times the old Corn Exchange had to be extended, in order to cope with the business. After the repeal of the Corn Laws in 1849, the importation of corn increased at such a prodigious rate that the existing building became practically use-

40

less. A scheme for a rival Corn Exchange was brought out, and upon this the proprietors of the old building, taking alarm, pulled it down and rebuilt it upon a greatly extended scale. This was in 1851.

The name of one street in Liverpool, Redcross Street, has always puzzled local antiquarians, since no record can be found of any cross or monument in the neighbourhood from which the name could have been taken. An obelisk covering a cistern and a pump, called Tarleton's Obelisk, was erected near by in 1763 by John Tarleton, mayor in that year, but it was never called a cross. Redcross Street was begun about the end of the seventeenth century, and at first it was the residence of wealthy merchants, but from the middle to the end of the eighteenth century it was the Bold Street of its time, the leading shops of the town being interspersed among the large private houses, one of which, so late as 1803, was occupied by the then mayor, Mr. Jonas Bold. The Crown Inn on the north side of the street was for many years one of the principal coaching establishments in Liverpool, especially for the north road service, no less than sixteen departures a day being advertised in the *Directory* for 1805. Before the street was made, the ground on which it stood was called " Tarleton's Field."

Reference has already been made to the old Town Hall. It also served as an exchange. The last mention of the original building was in 1617 when a tax was levied on the inhabitants for the " repayre of bridges and of the Town-Hall." In Richard Blome's *Magna Britannia*, which was published in 1673 and contains a description of the principal towns of the kingdom, we find this interesting account of the progress of Liverpool, and of the successor to the thatched

building which had housed the mayor, the town prisoners, and served for the deliberations of the Town Council :—" It (Liverpool) is of late, at the great charge and industry of the family of the Mores of Bank Hall, beautified with many goodly buildings all of hewn stone, much to the honour and advancement of the said town ; which family of the Mores, for some hundreds of years, have had a large property therein, and at present continue chief lords and owners of the greatest share thereof, having divers streets that bear their name, intirely of their inheritance ; which hath so enlarged the town, that its church is not enough to hold its inhabitants, which are many ; amongst which are divers eminent merchants and tradesmen, whose trade and traffic, especially in the West Indies, makes [it famous ; its situation affording in greater plenty, and at reasonable rates, than most parts of England, such exported commodities proper for the West Indies ; as likewise a quicker return for such imported commodities, by reason of the sugar bakers, and great manufacturers of cottens [1] in the adjacent parts, and the rather for that it is found to be the convenient passage to Ireland, and divers considerable counties in England with which they have intercourse of traffick. Here is now erected at the publick charge of the Mayor and Aldermen, etc., a famous town house, placed on pillars and arches of hewen stone, and underneath it is the publick exchange for the merchants. It hath a very considerable market on Saturdays for all sorts of provisions and divers commodities which are brought by the merchants, and thence transported as aforesaid."

This second Town Hall or Exchange

[1] Lancashire "cottens" were then coarse woollen fabrics, the word being probably a corruption of "coatings."

41

after being the centre of Liverpool's municipal and commercial life for some seventy-five years began to show signs of decay. In this period the town had made such an advance in commerce, in wealth Baltic, Mediterranean, Coasting, and Virginia, the foundation stone being laid in September 1749. Five years later the building was opened with public rejoicings which lasted a whole week, with

REDCROSS STREET

and in population that it was decided to erect a building more in keeping with its importance. The Royal Exchange in London was taken as a model, with two arcades and six walks across for the following trades—Irish, West India, public breakfasts every morning, boat-races during the days, and balls and concerts every evening. It was a great moment in the history of Liverpool.

Of the Liverpool of 1760, its new Exchange, and the Liverpool merchants, we are given a glimpse by no less a person than a Master of the Ceremonies at Bath —Samuel Derrick—in *Letters written from Liverpool, Chester, Cork, etc.* After describing the river and the docks, which were then only three in number, he says, "The docks are flanked with broad, commodious quays, surrounded by handsome brick houses, inhabited for the most part by sea-faring people, and communicating with the town by drawbridges and floodgates, which a man must be wary in crossing over, as they are pretty narrow." Then he writes of the Exchange and what went on there:—"The Exchange is a handsome square structure of grey stone supported by arches. Being blocked up on two sides with old houses, it is so very dark that little or no business can be transacted in it ; but the merchants assemble in the street opposite to it, as they used to before it was erected, and even a heavy shower can scarcely drive them to a harbour. In the upper part are noble apartments, wherein the corporation transact public business. The court-room is remarkably handsome, large and commodious, here the mayor tries petty causes, and has power to sentence for transportation. The assembly-room, which is also upstairs, is grand, spacious, and finely illuminated ; here is a meeting once a fortnight to dance and play cards ; where you will find some women elegantly accomplished and perfectly well dressed. The proceedings are regulated by a lady styled ' the Queen,' and she rules with very absolute power."

Such praise of the Liverpool ladies from so great an arbiter of fashion as the Master of the Ceremonies at Bath was praise indeed. Having complimented the ladies, Mr. Samuel Derrick next turns his attention to the gentlemen. "Though few of the merchants," he says, "have had more education than befits a counting-house, they are genteel in their address. They are hospitable, nay friendly, even to those of whom they have the least possible knowledge. Their tables are plenteously furnished, and their viands well served up ; their rum is excellent, of which they consume large quantities, made, when the West India fleets come in, mostly with times, which are very cooling, and afford a delicious flavour. But they pique themselves greatly upon their ale, of which almost every house brews a sufficiency for its own use ; and such is the unanimity prevailing amongst them, that if by accident one man's stock runs short, he sends his pitcher to his neighbour to be filled. Though I am not very fond of the beverage usually prepared under that name, I learnt from the peculiar excellency of this to like it a little. I must add, that I drank some of a superior quality with Mr. Mears,[1] a merchant in the Portuguese trade ; his malt was bought at Derby, his hops in Kent, and his water brought by express order from Lisbon."

In these days of universal peace it is curious to read that Liverpool owed much of her prosperity to being able to undersell her neighbours because her vessels paid less insurance for war-risks. Mr. Derrick continues, "The principal exports of Leverpoole are all kinds of woollen and worsted goods, with other manufactures of Manchester and Yorkshire, Sheffield and Birmingham wares, etc. These they barter on the coast of Guinea for slaves, gold dust, and elephants' teeth. These slaves they dispose of at Jamaica, Barbadoes, and the other West India islands for rum and sugar, for which they are sure of a quick sale at home. This port is admirably suited for trade, being almost central in the channel ; so that in war time, by coming north about, their ships

[1] This was Mr. Thomas Mears, who lived in Paradise Street.

have a good chance of escaping the many privateers belonging to the enemy, which cruise to the southward. Thus, their insurance being less, they are able to undersell their neighbours; and since I have been here I have seen enter the port in

widening of Castle Street, and other improvements in the neighbourhood, a feeling became general amongst the merchants that better accommodation was needed for the transaction of their ever-growing business than that afforded by the old

THE SECOND "NEW" EXCHANGE

one morning, seven West India ships, whereof five were not insured."

In 1795, the whole of the interior of the Exchange was destroyed by fire; the restoration was not completed until two years afterwards. The Act for the improvement of Liverpool, passed in 1786, had made a considerable difference in the appearance of the town, and after the

Exchange. The feeling grew, and when, in 1801, a project for the building of an Exchange to be devoted exclusively to commerce was brought forward, the subscription list of eighty thousand pounds was filled up in three hours, although no person could take more than ten shares. Two years later the foundation stone was laid, and in 1808 it was opened to the

44

public. During the visit of the Prince Regent and his brother the Duke of Clarence to Liverpool in 1806, the exterior of the building was already completed and they were driven in a coach round the arcades, this being the only occasion in which horse or carriage ever passed beneath them. For fifty years the second "New" Exchange served the Liverpool merchants, then it was found that it was all too small. History had repeated itself. The proprietors refusing to enlarge the building, a new company was formed in 1862. An Act of Parliament was obtained, which authorised the buying out of the old company, the pulling down of the Exchange, and its rebuilding upon a larger scale. The old proprietors, under an award, were given £317,350; in order that the Exchange might be extended westward £60,000 was paid for the site of the old Sessions House, and, in addition to these sums, £220,000 was spent upon the building.

The Old Fort at Liverpool was only in existence some thirty years. It was erected in 1778, when England was at war with France, Spain and America at one and the same time, a most formidable coalition. It stood on the north shore, near the bottom of Denison Street,

THE OLD FORT

barracks being built near it for the accommodation of the "Liverpool Blues," a regiment raised and equipped in the town chiefly at the expense of the Corporation. In May 1778, mustering eleven hundred strong, the Liverpool Blues were reviewed on the sands near Bank Hall and presented with their colours. Three weeks later they were sent on active service from which only eighty-four returned in 1784 (from Jamaica). Their colours were deposited in the Exchange. After the departure of the Blues the town was garrisoned by a regiment of Yorkshire

45

G

ST. HELENS AND PLATE=GLASS

WHEN one remembers the countless chimneys of the plate-glass works at St. Helens, the wide area they cover, and the number of men they employ, it is difficult to realise the description given by a visitor to the town in 1840. "The staple manufacture of the place is plate-glass, which is carried on at Ravenhead, and is the largest establishment of the kind in England, affording employment for more than three hundred workmen. The establishment at Ravenhead covers about thirty acres of ground, and is enclosed by a lofty stone wall, and secured by gates. Beyond the wall are the cottages occupied by the workpeople, which are for the most part neat and convenient, though not quite equal in comfort and appearance to the cottages of operatives in other parts of Lancashire."

The manufacture of plate-glass was first begun at St. Helens in 1773, when the British Cast Plate-Glass manufactory was founded. But its originators were obliged to bring workpeople over from France, the method of manufacturing big sheets of glass being unknown in England. The venture failed, and in 1798, a new company was formed, called the British Plate-Glass Company. This was an immediate success, and led the way to St. Helens becoming the principal seat of the plate-glass manufacture in the country.

We learn in our school-books that glass is a compound of silex and alkali, fused together by intense heat; also that silex is flint or sand, and the principal alkalis are potash and soda. Silex under ordinary circumstances cannot be melted alone, and a "flux" is therefore needed—some substance that will liquefy more readily than the material primarily designed to be melted, and the action of which will render it more sensible to the operation of heat. In the melting of metals difficult of fusion "fluxes" are invariably used, but after the operation is concluded they are generally separated again from the metal. But in the manufacture of glass the alkali forms both the "flux" and an ingredient, helping to melt the silex and combining with it. For plate-glass soda is preferred for the "flux," and as this is obtained from common salt—the chemical name of which is muriate of soda—the plentiful supply of this article from the Cheshire salt-works, and the abundance of coal, led to St. Helens being chosen for the first plate-glass manufactory in England.

The discovery that glass is made by the fusion of silex and an alkali goes far back into the days of antiquity. We are told that some mariners being driven by stress of weather into the mouth of the River Belus on the coast of Phœnicia, where the plant kali grew in abundance, kindled a fire on the shore to cook their food. The ashes of the kali plant were incorporated with the silicious sand on the river bank by the heat, and to their amazement the sailors found transparent stones where their fire had been. The truth of this anecdote has been questioned on the ground that specimens of glass have been found in some of the oldest Egyptian tombs; but there was active intercourse between the Egyptians and the Phœnicians, and for centuries the sands of the Belus were famous throughout the then civilised world as being the best obtainable for the making of glass. During the golden period of the Roman Empire, Sidon and Alexandria were celebrated for their manufacture of fine glass, and both the Tyrians and the Egyptians used the sand from the shores of the Belus. In the Middle Ages Venice had almost the complete monopoly for the making of fine glass, but the Venetian glass was blown and therefore only of small size. The method of casting large plates of glass for windows and for mirrors was started in France towards the close of the seventeenth century by a man

MARK OF THE BRITISH CAST PLATE-GLASS MANUFACTORY 1773

called Thévart, and until the founding of the English company at St. Helens in 1773, French glass of this kind held the market. As we have seen, French workmen were brought over, and having learnt the process from them, the St. Helens manufacturers improved upon it so rapidly that in a short while British plate-glass became superior to that of any other country.

But, before the British Plate-Glass Company had perfected the manufacture, the action of light on plate-glass long exposed to the rays of the sun was very remarkable. The glass acquired a violet or purple tinge which may still be seen in the windows of old houses. This was caused by some chemical used in the mixture. The effect of light upon the chemical was discovered by exposing portions of a plate to the air for some months, other portions being covered over. The difference between them became so great that it was difficult to believe that the exposed and the unexposed portions had ever been one and the same plate.

Here we have a picture of 1840—a vivid contrast with the vast buildings of to-day:—

"The furnace in which the glass is melted occupies the centre of a large building called the Foundry. The foundry at Ravenhead is the largest apartment under one roof in Great Britain, being one hundred and thirteen yards in length, by a little over fifty in breadth. The glass is fused in earthen pots or crucibles, which are placed in the central furnace, and exposed to the most intense heat. They have not only to endure the action of the fire, but also the solvent power of the glass itself, and of the fluxes which are used for liquefying the silex. In fact, the best crucibles gradually dissolve and mix a portion of their earth with the glass which they contain, and hence it is necessary not only that they should be composed of materials difficult to fuse, but also of earths sufficiently pure not to injure the glass should a portion of them combine with it. The crucibles or pots are com-

MARK OF THE BRITISH PLATE-GLASS COMPANY 1798

monly made of five parts of the finest Stourbridge clay and one part of old crucibles ground to powder. These materials are kneaded together by the feet

47

of the workmen, a process which it has been found impossible to supersede by machinery.

"The materials are prepared for the crucibles by a process called 'fritting.' They are calcined together by being exposed to a degree of heat sufficient to bring them to a consistence like paste. All moisture is thus effectually removed ; for a drop of water in the materials, or a globule of air in the crucibles, would by its expansion produce an injurious explosion in the furnace. The carbonic acid in the alkalis and chalk is at the same time expelled, and an amalgamation of the different materials begins to take place, which gives uniformity to the subsequent process of melting. The 'frit' is cut into square cakes, and put into the crucibles in successive portions until they are quite filled. This is rather a tedious operation because the 'frit' is more bulky than the fused metal, and no new portion can be added until the preceding charge is melted down. As the materials melt and fuse together, an opaque white scum rises to the surface, which is carefully skimmed away. This scum is called 'glass-gall' and is useful as a flux to the refiners of metals. If not removed, the glass-gall would be volatised, and in its form of vapour greatly injure the furnace and the crucibles. As the heat continues the glass-gall disappears, and the glass throws to its surface minute bubbles, which burst on the top and become beautifully brilliant. The process from the cessation of the vapour of the glass-gall to the time when no more bubbles are thrown up, is called 'refining.' When it terminates, the metal has become uniformly clear, transparent and colourless ; and it is tested by taking out samples with an iron rod and allowing them to cool. When the glass is thoroughly refined, it is transferred in its liquid state from the pots or crucibles into a vessel or cistern. When this vessel was small it was called a *cuvette*, when large, a *mullion*, both French terms introduced by the original French workmen. This transfer is effected by means of a copper ladle about a foot in diameter, fixed into an iron handle seven feet long. As the cistern has been previously heated to a temperature equal to that of the glass, there is obviously a great danger that the copper would give way under the great heat and weight of the melted glass. To prevent such an accident, the bottom of the ladle is supported by an iron bar held by two other workmen. This process is one of the most severe on the persons employed, both on account of the heat and the fatigue. After the cistern has been filled it must remain for several hours in the furnace, that the air-bubbles which were formed by pouring the liquid metal from one vessel to another should have time to rise and disperse. In many of the olden mirrors it is not unusual to find one or two air flaws, which greatly disfigure the plate, and render the reflection imperfect. The metal in the cistern is examined by taking out samples until it is ascertained that all the air-bubbles have been dispersed, and it is then ready to be removed to the casting-table."

The casting-table in use in France and also at the Ravenhead Foundry was made of copper and supported by solid masonry, it being supposed that copper would have less effect in discolouring the hot melted glass than iron. But the British Plate-Glass Company found that copper was liable to crack under the sudden heat of a molten mass of liquid fire, and that over and over again, after a vast expense had been incurred in grinding and polishing the copper casting-tables, they cracked during the first time of use.

They therefore determined to try cast-iron. "It was not easy," continues the description of the manufactory in 1840, "to obtain an iron plate of the dimensions they required; but at length they were able to cast one, fifteen feet in length, nine in diameter, and six inches in thickness. This massive table, including its frame, weighs fourteen tons; and it was necessary to construct a carriage purposely for its conveyance from the iron foundry to the glass-house. It is supported on castors, for the convenience of readily removing it towards the mouths of the different annealing ovens. These ovens are placed in two rows on each side of the foundry, and are each sixteen feet wide, and forty feet deep. Their floors are exactly on the level of the casting-table. Notwithstanding the vast size of the apartment in which these operations are conducted, the greatest precautions are necessary to prevent any disturbance of the atmosphere from the time that a casting is commenced until the surface of the glass is hardened. The opening or shutting of a door, or a current of air through a window, would produce a disturbance of the atmosphere which would ripple the surface of the plate and impair its value. Hence it is very rarely that strangers are permitted to view this operation. When by inspection of the samples it is found that the melted glass in the cistern is in that state which experience has shown to be most favourable to its flowing readily and equally a signal is given, to ensure the perfect tranquillity necessary to the complete success of the operation. The cistern is then drawn from the furnace and removed to the casting-table, which has been previously heated with hot ashes and perfectly cleaned. The melted glass also is carefully skimmed to remove any impurities which may have collected on the surface; for the mixture of any foreign substance would infallibly spoil the plate. As soon as this is done the cistern is raised by a crane, so as to be at a small height above the upper end of the casting-table. It is then tilted over, and the melted glass pours like a flood of fire, flowing and spreading in every direction upon the table between two iron ribs; the intervals between each determine its breadth, and their height above the table its thickness. While the glass is still fluid, or nearly so, a heavy copper roller, turned very true in a lathe, passes over it resting on the ribs by which it is confined, and it rolls out the glass into an equable thickness through its entire length. Should the cistern contain more melted glass than is necessary to fill the table, the surplus is received in a vessel of water placed at the extreme end for the purpose; but if the glass falls short of the required quantity a movable rib is shifted up the table, so as to give a square termination to the plate and prevent unnecessary waste. Those who have seen this operation describe it as very splendid and interesting. The flow of the molten glass over the metallic table appears like a lava flood issuing from a volcano. The plate, as the copper passes over it, exhibits a great variety of rich hues, and the gradual disappearance of these as the metal cools is one of the most beautiful optical effects that can be produced. This operation requires the aid of about twenty workmen, each of whom has his particular duty assigned to him."

The difference between to-day and 1840, is even more clearly exemplified by the pride with which the writer refers to a sheet of plate-glass in the Reform Club in London, which measured twelve feet six inches by seven feet six inches, and was "supposed to be the most perfect in the world."

As soon as the plates were sufficiently cooled they were "pushed by main force" from the table into the annealing oven, being spread out in an horizontal position. When an oven was filled it was closed by an iron door and all the crevices stopped with clay, until the annealing process was complete. This took about fourteen or fifteen days. At the first fixed horizontally. A sheet of tin-foil, rather larger than the plate, is spread and carefully smoothed. As much quicksilver, in its liquid form, is then spread over the foil as will lie steadily on its surface without overflowing; and a linen cloth, the width of the plate of glass, is spread on that end of the table. The plate is then brought to the table

THE OLD CASTING-TABLE

end of this interesting account comes a description of the way in which mirrors were made in 1840. "This is a very simple operation, but great nicety and dexterity are requisite in the manipulation. A table of slate or stone is provided: round this table there is a groove or channel to carry off the surplus quicksilver; and the table rests on a pivot, so that it can, when necessary, be changed from a horizontal into an inclined plane. This slab or table is and made to slide steadily on to the foil charged with quicksilver. Great care is required in this operation, because the plate must dip in the quicksilver and push the metal before it, in order to remove any impurities or oxides which may rest on the surface of the quicksilver, and also to prevent the formation of air-bubbles between the amalgam and the plate; but at the same time it is necessary to prevent the plate from coming into immediate contact with the sheet of the foil, which would infallibly be torn by the slightest touch. When the entire plate has been brought into its position, and has dropped gently on the foil, it is heavily loaded with weights covered with flannel, to squeeze out the superfluous quicksilver, the escape of which is further facilitated by giving the slab a gentle slope, and increasing the inclination by slow degrees. A day or two afterwards the plate is carefully lifted up and turned over; its under side is thus covered over with a very soft amalgam made by the quicksilver and the foil. Several days, however, elapse before the amalgam has acquired the proper degree of hardness: and during this period globules of quicksilver drop from the lower edge of the plate. So long as the amalgam is in an imperfect state, portions of it are liable to be detached from it by any electrical changes in the atmosphere, or violent concussions of the air, such as a thunderstorm, a very high wind, or the firing of artillery. It is impossible to apply an adequate remedy to such an accident, for patching is immediately detected by the white seam which marks the line of contact between the old and the new amalgam. In most cases, where an imperfection is detected, the amalgam is removed and the process of silvering repeated from the very beginning."

All this was in 1840. Writing of St. Helens twenty-eight years later, Baines in his *History of Lancashire*, says: " In this district one-half of the glass made in England is manufactured, one-fourth of the alkali, and one-fourth of the copper; the gross value of these articles manufactured in St. Helens, and of the coal raised there, being more than three millions sterling annually, while the weekly wages paid are twenty thousand pounds. The manufactories of glass include four plate or cast glass, one crown and sheet or blown window glass, two flint and four bottle-glass works. The plate-glass works make three-fourths, the crown and sheet one-third, and the flint and bottles one-tenth, of all such glass made in England. The St. Helens Railway, which forms one-fortieth of the London and North Western Railway Company's mileage, conveys two million tons, or one-seventh of their entire traffic."

These figures afford an interesting comparison with those of to-day.

REJECTED OF LIVERPOOL

THOMAS THORNELEY was a striking instance of the prophet without honour in his own country —at least the honour he himself desired, and which was fully accorded him elsewhere. He was a Liverpool merchant, and, until his death in 1863, lived in a house in Mount Street, near the Liverpool Institute. Having made a modest fortune by the time he reached middle life, Thorneley retired from business and devoted his time to the affairs of the town. As early as 1817, we find Thorneley attending a meeting in Clayton Square, to petition the Prince Regent and the Houses of Parliament against the further suspension of the Habeas Corpus Act; in 1826 he was a speaker at a public meeting held in the Town Hall, under the presidency of the Mayor, to urge the repeal of the Corn Laws; in 1831 he addressed a meeting "to consider the propriety of again petitioning both Houses of Parliament on the subject of opening the trade to China and India," and a few months later spoke in the cause of Reform at another public meeting.

The Reform Bill was then agitating the whole country, and upon this burning question the election of 1831 was fought at Liverpool. Mr. Ewart and Mr. Denison were returned, in spite of the latter declining to stand. In the same election

Thornley.

Mr. Denison was elected for Nottinghamshire, and, preferring to sit for that county, another contest became necessary in Liverpool, and the more advanced section of the Whigs chose Thorneley as their candidate. The Tories and the moderate Whigs invited Lord Sandon (afterwards Earl of Harrowby) to come forward. Meetings were held by both sides, but it speedily became evident that Lord Sandon was the popular candidate. Thorneley did not possess the gifts which impress the mob. He was not a good speaker, but his absolute honesty inspired confidence and respect. His speeches were marked by a simple directness and a thorough acquaintance with his subject which are of little avail in impressing meetings inflamed by political passions. In person he was stately, and had most courteous old-world manners. Lord Sandon, on the other hand, was young, he was an agreeable "rattle," and above all was surrounded by the glamour of aristocracy. Whilst canvassing amongst the tenants of St. John's Market, the noble candidate in the most gallant and debonair fashion kissed a pretty market-woman called Hetty Taylor. This tribute to local beauty roused tremendous enthusiasm, and immediately afterwards the following dialogue, put forth by the other side, was sold all over the town :—

His Lordship. O peerless market-queen, fair
Hetty!
Deign to bestow on me a kiss ;
And if your charming daughter Betty
Would do the same—'twould crown my
bliss.
Hetty (with a blush and a curtsey). Thank you,
my lord, with all my heart,
You're kindly welcome to a kiss ;
Betty and I will take your part,
You may do what you please with us.
His Lordship. Oh, Hetty, dear, my hopes
'twould crown,
If women young and fair prove steady,
For all *old women* in the town
Are in my interest already.
Hetty. Keep up your heart, for (barring
slips)
I swear your cause I'll ne'er abandon.
His Lordship. Let's seal the contract on
those lips.
Hetty. With all my heart—" Huzza for
Sandon."

At previous elections there had been
wholesale bribing of the " freemen," and,
pending a Parliamentary inquiry, the
writ for the fresh election was suspended.
The writ was not granted until October
12, and in the meantime no meetings
could be held ; but Thorneley's supporters
very cleverly took advantage of a public
dinner given in honour of King William
IV.'s birthday, by making it into a demon-
stration on his behalf. The election took
place on October 20, Thorneley polling
only 670 votes against Lord Sandon's

1,519, an immense sensation being caused
by a prominent supporter of Thorneley's
making a bitter attack upon him during
the " chairing" of Lord Sandon. He
described the defeated candidate as an
utterly incapable person, who had not
even the ability to address a public meeting. It was a cruel and undeserved
attack.

In the following year the great Reform
Bill was passed, which necessitated
another election ; this time Thorneley
came out third in the poll with 4,096
votes. He had been induced to stand a
second time by the tradesmen of Liverpool. Two years later Wolverhampton
sought him as its member, and returning
him triumphantly to Westminster, kept
him there for twenty years. " His connection with this borough," says Mr.
Picton, " was equally honourable to himself and his constituents, they having the
good sense rightly to appreciate his
sterling worth." Thorneley was much
respected by both sides in the House of
Commons, and served on many important
committees. He retired from Parliament
in 1859, owing to age and increasing
infirmities, and died at his house in
Mount Street, Liverpool, in 1863. The
services twice rejected by Liverpool proved
of signal advantage to Wolverhampton.

SPEKE HALL

SPEKE HALL is one of the finest specimens of the Elizabethan manor-house in Lancashire, and, like so many of its fellows in the county, it has passed through many vicissitudes of ownership after the families which built and adorned them have died out.

Speke came to the Norris family in the reign of Edward I., by marriage with an heiress. This family has been settled in Lancashire from a very early period, but the first amongst them to gain renown was Sir William Norris, who was slain in the Scottish war during the reign of Henry VIII. This Sir William, in one of the English raids into Scotland, brought away part of the royal library at Holy-rood as well as a quantity of curious wainscoting, as his share of booty. The wainscoting was put up in the hall at Speke by his son Sir Edward Norris, who likewise was a distinguished soldier and commanded a large body of men under

Sir Edward Stanley at the Battle of Flodden. From the fact that the son placed the Holyrood wainscoting in the hall at Speke, his father's prowess in sacking the palace of the Scottish king has been attributed to him. Seccombe, in his fulsome *History of the House of Stanley*, was doubtless responsible for the mistake, for he says, definitely, "This valiant and heroic gentleman, Sir Edward Norris, commanded a body of the army under General Stanley, at Flodden Field, where he behaved with so much courage and good conduct, that he was honoured by the king his master, with a like con-gratulatory letter (this refers to the letter sent by Henry VIII. to Sir Edward Stanley) for his good service in the victory of that day ; in token whereof he brought from the deceased King of Scots' palace, all or most of his princely library, many books of which are now at Speke, parti-cularly four large folios, said to contain the records and laws of Scotland at that time, and worthy of the perusal of the learned and judicious reader. And he also brought from the said palace, the wainscot of the king's hall, and put it up in his own hall at Speke."

But proof of the inaccuracy of Seccombe's story has been discovered in the Liverpool Athenæum. Fourteen folio-volumes were bought by the Athenæum at a sale, and in each volume, in crabbed sixteenth - century writing, is a record by Sir William Norris, himself. One of these, turned into modern English, says, that "Edinburgh was won the 8th day of May in the 36th year of Henry VIII. and in the year 1544, and that this book called 'Bartolus sup. prim' Degesti veteris,' was gotten and brought away by me William Norris of the Speke, knight, the 11th day of May aforesaid, and now the book of me the aforesaid Sir William, given and by me left to remain at Speke for an heirloom. In witness whereof I have written this with my own hand and subscribed my name. me. William Norris, knight."

Sir Edward Norris placed the famous Holyrood wainscoting upon the northern wall of the great hall at Speke. It is divided into forty panels, each of which, with the exception of every fourth one, has a carved grotesque head. In the fourth panel are oval shields supported by two lions. These appear to have been meant for armorial bearings. In the second row of panels the following inscription is carved in detached portions in old English characters :—

"Slepe not till ye hath well considered how thow has spent the day past. If thow have well don thank God. If otherways, repent ye."

Over the mantelpiece in the drawing-room there is a carved pedigree in oak of three generations of the Norris family,

and above the superbly carved doorway of the same room is another of those admonitory inscriptions which our Elizabethan forbears delighted to have carved about their houses :—

"The streghtest waye to Heaven ys God to love and serve above all thyng."

From the time of Elizabeth, when the present house was built, until the reign of William III., the Norrises led the lives of country gentlemen. Towards the close of the seventeenth century the then owner, Sir William Norris, who had represented Liverpool in three successive Parliaments, married the daughter of a London alderman, Sir John Garraway, and through his father-in-law's influence was chosen as Ambassador to the Great Mogul at Delhi.

Already in the reign of William III., the power of the East India Company was causing some anxiety to the authorities, and a new Company was projected, not only as a rival but to supersede the old one. With a view to establishing friendly relations between the new Company and the then Emperor of India, Sir William Norris was dispatched at the head of a splendid retinue, provided with ample funds, and all that would be likely to impress an Eastern potentate. But through the intrigues of the agents of the old East India Company, Sir William's embassy failed completely, and broken in health and utterly discomfited he was obliged to return. He died on the voyage back to England. A relic of his embassy, which shows the dignity with which it was invested, is preserved at Liverpool. It is a sword, and was presented by the Norris family to the Liverpool Corporation ; and is thus inscribed :—

"This sword of state carried before his Excellency Sir William Norris, of Speke, in his embassy to the great Mogul, given as a memorial of respect to this Corporation. Anno Domini 1702. John Cockshutt Mayor."

With the death of Sir William's son the ancient family of Norris came to an end in the male line, and Speke descended to his granddaughter, Mary Norris, who in 1736 married Lord Sidney Beauclerk, a son of the Duke of St. Albans, who in his turn was the son of Charles II. and Nell Gwynne. Beauclerk was described as a "notorious fortune-hunter"; he was a gambler and a spendthrift. The last of the Norrises of

Speke had a wretched married life. Their son, Topham Beauclerk, was a great figure in London society, especially in literary and artistic circles. He was the friend of Dr. Johnson and of Sir Joshua Reynolds. But he, too, was a spendthrift, and Speke, already heavily mortgaged with the rest of the property, was sold. It was bought by a man named Watt, who had been a stable boy in a Liverpool inn. He went out to the West Indies, where he made a large fortune, and returning home became a rich merchant in Liverpool.

AN OLD BILL OF LADING

IN the more leisurely times of a hundred and twenty years ago, Liverpool merchants used a very different form for their bills of lading than those in use to-day. In the following bill the words in italics are written, the remainder is in copper-plate printing.

Shipped by the Grace of God and in good order and condition by Sydebotham & Harrocks in and upon the good ship called The *Sutton*, whereof is master (under God) for this present voyage, *Samuel Lee*, and now riding at anchor in the river Mersey, and by God's grace bound for *Dublin* to-day *Two bales of merchandise*

being marked and numbered as in the margin, and are to be delivered in the like good order and condition at the aforesaid port of *Dublin* (the danger of the seas only excepted) with *Messrs Oxley and Hague and Arthur Annesley, Merchants* there, or to their assigns, the assigns, or they, paying freight for the said goods, *four pence per ton*. In witness whereof the Master or purser of the said ship hath affirmed to three bills of lading, all of this tenor and date; the one of which three bills being accomplished, the other two stand void. And so God send the good ship to her desired haven in safety. Amen. Dated in Liverpool 16 *November* 1790.

Samuel Lee

N

56

FOLLY FAIR AT LIVERPOOL

THE FOLLY

I T is difficult to believe that so late as the end of the eighteenth century the heath came close to where St. George's Hall now stands. But on an old print a triangular area to the north of the Hall shows as rough land, with a wooden windmill in the centre. The mill was taken down about 1780, and the ground levelled and paved, and here Folly Fair was held on Easter Monday and Easter Tuesday each year, the origin of the festivity and its name arising thus. A short distance up what is now called Islington, but was then the only road to West Derby, and near the site of the present Christian Street, a tea-house with a strawberry garden about it was kept by a man called Gibson, who was likewise the lessee and manager of the Theatre

Royal. On to the tea-house he built a great square tower, eight storeys in height, apparently as a gazebo or look-out, since the situation commanded a considerable and extensive view.

Whatever the reason for the erection of this curious structure it was popularly called "Gibson's Folly," and the road which led to it in the course of time became known as Folly Lane. In those times "lifting" was common at Easter in Liverpool, the men "lifting" the women on Easter Monday, the women "lifting" the men on Easter Tuesday. As recorded elsewhere this custom was of great antiquity, and in the early days was symbolical of the Resurrection. "Within the memory of many persons now living," says Mr. Picton, writing in 1875, "it was

N 2

impossible for a female to pass through any of the lower streets of Liverpool on Easter Monday without being laid hold of by a set of good-natured ruffians, who asked for 'backsheesh,' and if it was not granted, she was taken by the head and heels and heaved three times in the air. On Easter Tuesday the females retaliated, and many a 'grave and reverend signior' has had to run for it; to pay toll, or to be seized by a posse of stalwart women who were not over particular in handling him."

Gradually a sort of fair grew up around the Folly Gardens, "lifting" playing a large part on both days. The "Folly" itself was pulled down about 1780, the tea-garden and house having been purchased by Mr. Philip Christian, who built himself a large house on the site, and Folly Fair then took place on the open piece of ground mentioned above. As the population of Liverpool grew, so the Fair increased in proportion each year, but gradually it became a saturnalia of drunkenness, debauchery and fighting. Respectable folk held aloof, and it became the resort of the lowest kind of roughs. Each year notices and proclamations were issued forbidding the Fair, but the small police force at the disposal of the authorities made it impossible for them to carry their proclamations into effect, and they were openly disregarded. At last matters became so serious, and the scandal so flagrant, that the space in 1818 was turned into a market, called Islington Market, the space being enclosed with brick walls and iron gates, with rows of small shops round the interior. Folly Fair was therefore transferred to the open fields on the north side of the London Road, now covered by Stafford Street, but it did not bear transplanting, and in a year or two came to an end. Public opinion in Liverpool had undergone a great change in forty years; nevertheless there were those who regretted the discontinuance of the Fair, as is witnessed by these lines, published in a Liverpool paper at the time :—

A LAMENT FOR FOLLY FAIR.

" Breathers of harmony, who oft of yore
Vouchsafed your aid alike to joy and grief,
O deign t' assist my sad and mournful lay ;
To touch the flinty and unfeeling hearts
Of those whose harsh, imperious edicts
Have doomed thy woeful fall, O FOLLY FAIR !
O let each gentle nymph, who at the approach
Of soft-eyed spring has loved to wander there,
And sport her gay attire 'midst fragrant groves
Of oranges, raise her melodious voice
In sweet but sighing cadence—let the swain
In whose fond bosom must for ever dwell
The dear remembrance of the blissful hours
Which he experienced, when upon his arm
The smiling fair one pressed with welcome weight,
Much wondering at the things she saw and heard—
Let him assay to raise a dolorous stave
Of grief and desolation. Ye who dwell
By the wayside in habitations frail,
But furnished well with toys, and fruit and cakes,
Uplift your voices, not as you were wont,
Shrilly and sharply, but wailingly and low,
And, if you can let fall a pearly tear,
So much the better. Princes and Potentates
Who hold your courts in moving palaces,
Strip off your glittering robes, your awful hands
Unsceptre, for your glory is laid low.
Thou Merry Andrew, show forth thy distress,
In horrible grimaces, kick thy heels
Aloft in air, in token that thy power
Is vanished ; ye double-headed calves
With bellowing loud, proclaim your mighty woe.

Ye dancing bears join all your deep-toned
   voices,
Till the loud strain reverberate around.
Ye, by whose touch the notes of melody
Are oft awakened, ye whose magic powers
Have oft sustained throughout the mid-
   night hour

Th' unwearied dancer, strike the deepest
   tones
To some most wild and lamentable lay,
For soon your harmony shall be laid low ;
Your sticks hang idly on the dusty wall,
While silence spreads her shadowy wing
   around."

George Day, Newsman,
Who, in his daily avocation is said to have
walked a distance exceeding the circum-
ference of the globe.

Hale Hall

THE Lancashire chronicler Randle Holme, writing of Hale Church in 1650, gives the epitaphs of three gravestones, then in the chancel. The first shows the power of the Pope in thirteenth-century England, and the antiquity of the building :—

" Here lies Master John Leyot, Bachelor of Decrees, dean of Chester, rector of the churches
of Malpas and Bangor, who first obtained this free burial-place from the supreme Pontiff Urban VI., at his own cost, at the Court of Rome, A.D. 1400 temp. Richard II.,
and to his soul God be gracious. Amen. Whosoever will say a pater noster and ave for
the good of his soul may have 300 days of indulgence."

There is a mistake in the date, as Richard II. reigned from 1377 to 1399, and Pope Urban VI. reigned from 1378 to 1389 ; the right of free burial at Hale would there-fore have been given between those two latter years.

The second epitaph read :—

" Here lies John Yerland Esq. who was lord of Hale and half the vill. of Lower Belington, who died 2ᵈ May, 1462, on whose
soul God have mercy. Amen."

Both of these tombs have disappeared, and only part of the inscription of John Yerland—the way of spelling Ireland—remains. He was one of the many owners of Hale who, between 1291 and 1626, passed on the estate from father to son.

The third tomb, which still remains, has a pathetic interest.

"Here lieth Sir Gilbert Ireland, knight, April 8th 1626. The last of his house. God's will be done."

Sir Gilbert was a man of note in Lancashire. He was Deputy Lieutenant of the county and built the front of Hale Hall. It was he, too, who took the Hale giant, the Child of Hale, to London in order that James I. might see this prodigy. The Irelands as Lords of Hale had curious rights. All wrecks, waifs and strays of the sea, and royal fish taken within the manor, were their property; anchorage money was also claimed at the rate of fourpence for every vessel casting anchor on the Lancashire side of the channel within the limits of the manor, or which shipped goods from Hale. Their tithe of the fish caught in the manor waters was afterwards commuted to all those caught on the Friday of each week.

There are some interesting entries in the Court Book of Hale, showing how these rights were enforced. In 1392 it was recorded : " John Colls was at Hale with a ship lying in Ladypull, and have bought and have taken 24 quarters of barley. Paid to Roger Robinson, bailiff of the manor, 4d., Sir John Ireland's Hale Toll according to the custom of the manor." Early in the next century we find " Persons presented (prosecuted) for fishing on the Domain ; all in Hale and Halewood fined for unlawful fishing in the several fisheries of the lord without license." In 1415, Thomas Smith, the chaplain, was fined for cutting wood; and a person was "presented" for refusing to sell ale to Thomas Leyot, and fined fourpence. Others were fined for stopping water-courses, not repairing their buildings, committing waste on the lands, for scolding, and for not

working in harvest-time. One man whose dog bit a sheep was fined tenpence. During the reign of Henry VI. an entry in the books shows how rigidly the manorial rights were enforced. " It happened within the lordship of Hale, on Saturday before the Feast of St. Luke (1435) after the hour of nine in the evening, that John Pogleden was in a boat or canoe upon the sea, and casually fell over the side of the canoe, and was drowned (to whose soul God be merciful) upon which it was presented that divers goods therein named were delivered by Roger Robinson, the bailiff, to Henry Pogleden, father of John, to keep to the use of the said lord, as wrecks of the sea ; and shortly after a frigate, or royal boat, was cast on shore, and seized as a wreck of the sea."

One tenth of the poultry, calves, lambs, goats, swine, fruits, cheese and butter of Hale went to the prior of Lancaster for food for the monks.

By virtue of good marriages the Irelands in the reign of Elizabeth held the manors of Hale, Hutt, Halewood and Halebank. The Earl of Derby was their over-lord, and to him they gave two roses every Midsummer Day, as a sign that they held the manor from him.

This is the description of Hale in the first half of the last century :—

" The village of Hale is one of the neatest and most rural in all this part of Lancashire. Being at a distance from any public road, and destitute of any manufactory, it is sequestered and peaceful. The cottages are healthy, thatched and whitewashed, while the handsome modern villa of the clergyman, built in 1824, and the venerable mansion formerly the parsonage house, though at present nothing more than a farm house, adorn the village green. The church yard is kept with much neatness, and is a charming retreat from the noise and bustle of the world. It is remote from the village and joins the park of Mr. Blackburn. The venerable hall of Hale the broad expanse of the Mersey, and the romantic hills above Frodsham in Cheshire, are objects seen to advantage from it."

Arms of Liverpool

THE SIEGES OF LIVERPOOL

IN the space of a little over a year Liverpool underwent three sieges. This was early in the struggle between Charles I. and the Parliament. The first siege took place in 1643, when Lord Molyneux retired to Liverpool after the Royalists had been worsted at Whalley. He was closely followed by the victorious Parliamentarian leader, Colonel Assheton, but before the latter's arrival Lord Molyneux had crossed into Cheshire, leaving a garrison in Liverpool. Colonel Assheton gained possession of the church, and placing his cannon upon the tower and his forces along the line of Dale Street, he cleverly drove the Royalists into the Castle. Here they offered a parley, proposing to surrender on condition that they should be allowed to retire with their arms and ammunition to join the royal forces. Assheton having them practically at his mercy, it was scarcely likely that he would assent to these conditions. His answer was a determined assault upon the Castle in which he " slew many of them, and put them into such confusion that as many as could, fled away for safety, and the rest were forced to yield themselves prisoners." Eighty of the Royalists were killed, three hundred were taken prisoners, and ten guns were captured.

Thus ended the first siege.

The Parliamentarians immediately put the place in a state of defence, Colonel Rosworm, the German engineer who had fortified Manchester, being brought down to strengthen and improve the Liverpool fortifications. At that time the line of Whitechapel and Paradise Street was the course of a stream that fed the Pool, and it being low marshy ground which was covered by the flood tides, batteries were erected at intervals to command the passage, and prevent any attack by boat. A rampart and a ditch extended from Dale Street westwards to Oldhall Street and the river, with strong gates where Tithebarn Street and Oldhall Street crossed one another. By the margin of the river a strong battery was erected, and cannon were mounted on the battlements of the Castle. By the 16th of May, 1643, all was ready ; the town was placed under martial law and Colonel John Moore appointed Governor. He was an active and vigilant commander, and it was at his suggestion, and partly at his expense, that several vessels were sent out for the purpose of blockading Dublin, and so to cut off supplies from the Royalist army in Ireland. That their services were effectual is shown by a letter from the Marquis of Ormonde to Lord Byron in January 1644, in which he says, " When the fleet is gone, it is too probable the Liverpool ships will look out again, if that town be not in the meantime reduced, which I most earnestly recommend your lordship to think of, and attempt, as soon as you possibly can, there being no service that to my apprehension can at once so much advantage this place (Dublin) and Chester, and make them so useful to each other."

Sir Thomas Powell had fortified the manor-house of Birkenhead for the King ; a small force was sent across the Mersey from Liverpool and took it for Parliament.

Although, by the spring of 1644, practically the whole of Lancashire was Parliamentarian, the heroic Countess of Derby alone holding out at Lathom House, the Governor of Liverpool had every reason to expect attack, as it was known that strong representations were being made to King Charles to raise the siege of Lathom House, and that in the event of this taking place a desperate effort would be made to regain Liverpool for the King. But notwithstanding the danger that threatened them the inhabitants did not take kindly to military duties and service upon the walls, since the Governor found it necessary to issue the following edict on May 25, 1644 :—

"Whereas divers of the inhabitants of this towne have refused and contemptuously neglected contrarie to divers orders to appeare with their best armes at the beating of the drum ; these are therefore to give publicke notice and warninge to all persons whatsoever inhabbiting within this garrison heretofore appoynted for the keeping of the watch within the same. That if they or any of them shall hereafter refuse or neglect to appeare at the beating of the drum for the settinge of the watch within the said garrison, or for the performing of other duties within the same ; or any person whatsoever sett upon his watch or guard shall come off the same or neglect his dutie therein, till he be called and releeved by an Officer—shall for everie such offence pay to the use of his fellow soldiers the sum of XIjd. (1s.) or lie in prison in the Townhall until he have paid the same."

Lack of observance of the Sabbath, however, was considered a more serious offence than a shirking of military duty, as witnesses this edict of January 28, 1644 :—

"It is ordered that all such householders or other persons as shall neglect the strict observance of Sundayes and fast dayes, and shall not frequent the church, but either loyter or stay abroad drinking, or shall be disorderly, and taken in anie misconduct, shall be severely punished, and shall forfeit for every offence 40s."

Toward the end of May 1644, Prince Rupert raised the siege of Lathom House after the terrible encounter between his troops and its former besiegers at Bolton, which has passed into history as "The Bolton Massacre"; and from Lathom he directed his attention upon Liverpool.

Reconnoitring the defences from the hills to the eastward of the town, Rupert pronounced the place to be indefensible— "a mere crow's nest which a parcel of boys might take"—but he nevertheless considered it necessary to build a line of batteries along what is now Lime Street, where, in the course of building, the trenches cut in the rock have been met with in comparatively recent times. Rupert met with an unexpectedly severe resistance.

He made his headquarters at Everton in a cottage which ever afterwards bore his name, and for eighteen days subjected the town to an incessant bombardment, in which he expended a hundred barrels of gunpowder. In addition to the bombardment repeated attacks were made upon the town, all of which were repulsed, the Royalists losing some fifteen hundred men. On June 17, 1644, this notice of the siege appeared in the *Mercurious Britannicus*: "The brave repulse which Colonel More, Governor of Liverpole, gave twice to Rupert (who assaulted that place with greate fury) is worthy of your notice. The seamen were very active in that service, and all are resolute to defend that place against Rupert, the Viper who devours his nourisher. 400 English and Scots are sent from Manchester to Warrington and thence by water to Liverpole, for their better assistance, and the Ships in the Harbour are well fitted to defend and make good a part of that town."

Prince Rupert fixed his camp round the Beacon, "a large mile from the Town," his officers being lodged in villages near. Twice each day men were brought from the camp to relieve those in the batteries and trenches, and to take part in the unsuccessful stormings. Bags of wool placed on the top of the mud walls were said to have saved the besieged from the hail of small shot showered upon them by the enemy.

At length, unable to carry the town by assaults in the day time, Prince Rupert decided on a night attack. The attacking force was led by Caryl, Lord Molyneux, who was thoroughly acquainted with the town, and an entrance was made by climbing the rampart where it joined tered all those they found in the streets, or who resisted them, until they reached the Cross, where they found the garrison drawn up in battle array. But these men offered no fight and, laying down their arms, demanded quarter, which was granted. They were, however, treated as prisoners of war, and were disposed of in the Tower, in St. Nicholas's Church and other places. The Royalist accounts state that all the ammunition and stores in the town fell into the hands of the victors ; but on the Parliamentarian side we have three stories, each of which gives the state-

A PERSPECTIVE VIEW OF OLD LIVERPOOL

the outhouses of Old Hall. One account says that the Prince was only enabled to enter the town by the wall on the north side having been deserted by its defenders, whilst another ascribes direct treachery to Colonel Moore: " I have heard say that Colonel Moor observing they wou'd be taken, he to ingratiate himself with the Prince, and to save his House and Effects at *Bank Hall* near it (the north wall) gave directions to the *Soldiers* to retreat from those Works." This can only have been the outcome of gossip, for Colonel Moore's fidelity and honour were never once questioned. On entering the town, the Royalists slaugh- ment a direct contradiction. The *Mercurious Britannicus* says : " Rupert hath at length with the number of his souldiers and continual assaults stormed the towne of Liverpoole, but the prudent Governor, with the losse of not above *sixty* men, kild him *fifteen* hundred, and finding that he could not hold the place any longer, he privately drew off his Ordnance, Armes and Ammunition, and afterwards his goods in the Towne, and safely conveyed them on board the Ships riding in the Poole, and disappointed *Rupert's* hopes therein." The two other accounts also give a very different complexion to the Royalist story of the garrison being granted quarter on their surrender. Whitelocke, a writer of the time, says: " Before the garrison surrendered, they shipped off all the arms, ammunition and portable effects; and most of the officers and soldiers went on shipboard, while a few made good the fort, which they surrendered to the prince upon quarter, but they were all put to the sword." Practically the same story is told in the *Discourse on the War in Lancashire*, in which the author says : " Colonell Moore, with what force he had with him in the towne, resisted while he could, but when he saw it was in vaine long to withstand such a potent army, he betook himself to the sea, and left the Towne to the mercilesse mercy of their enemies, who murthered inhumanly and plundered thevishly." And Edward Moore, the son of Colonel Moore, writing in his " rental " book twenty-three years after the siege, says with bitter feeling : " The outhouses of the Old Hall were pulled down when Prince Rupert took Liverpool, Whitsuntide, June 16, 1644, putting all to the sword for many hours, giving no quarter ; where Caryl, that is now Lord Molyneux, killed seven or eight poor men with his own hands. Good Lord, deliver us from the cruelty of bloodthirsty papists. Amen."

Prince Rupert stayed in Liverpool for nine days after taking the place, making his headquarters at the Castle. He then marched with all the available forces he could muster to raise the siege of York, but was utterly defeated by the Roundheads at Marston Moor and hotly pursued back again into Lancashire.

Lord Byron was left as Royalist governor in Liverpool. The thousand Parliamentary soldiers who were sent into Lancashire after the Battle of Marston Moor in pursuit of Prince Rupert were ordered to co-operate with the county forces, when they failed to secure him, with the result that an engagement took place at Ormskirk in which the Royalist generals, Lord Byron and Lord Molyneux, were defeated by the Roundhead Major-General Meldrum. The Royalists fell back upon Liverpool whither the Roundheads followed them, and, in military parlance, sat down before the town. This was the third siege, which lasted from August 20 to November 4, 1644. It was actually more of a blockade than a siege, for very little active fighting appears to have taken place, and few assaults, if any, to have been made by the besiegers. The Roundheads' object appears to have been to starve the Royalists into surrendering the town, which they on their side resisted to the uttermost. The following account of this desultory affair and its ending are given by a contemporary :—

" Sir John Meldrum having for some time laid siege to Liverpool in Lancashire, and reduced the garrison therein to great straits, and yet the officers refusing to surrender it, about fifty of the English soldiers escaped out of the town, and drove along with them what cattle they could, and came unto Meldrum ; which those that remained in the town perceiving, and being most of them Irish, and fearing they should be exempt from quarter, therefore to make their peace on November 1, they seized upon several of their commanders and delivered them prisoners to Meldrum, who thereupon got possession of the town, where there were taken two colonels, two lieutenant-colonels, three majors, fourteen captains, great store of ordnance, arms, and ammunition. The Royalists, to avoid plunder, had shipped most of their best goods and treasure "—doubtless in imitation of the course pursued by Colonel Moore—" intending to convey the same to Beaumaris, but those of the other party gave notice thereof, so that Meldrum's soldiers manned out long boats, and took and made booty thereof."

In the *Discourse on the War*, to which reference had already been made, the taking of the Royalist treasures is described " as a providence of God more than ordinary, for which Roundheads made bonfyres for joy and sung praises to God."

After this third siege Liverpool had peace, but during those troubled months when the town was thrown like a shuttlecock from one contending party to the other, the inhabitants had suffered severely. This entry on January 20, 1645, in the town records is significant of what had happened : " We find that a great company of our inhabitants were murthered and slain by Prince Rupert's forces ; the names of the murthered we cannot yet be certified of ; any of them or their names." By that time the mayor and council had been able to straighten the confusion into which borough affairs had fallen, and many burgesses and townsfolk were found to be missing. The next entry in the records goes to show that those who had been slain during the " hours of killing " in June 1644 by Rupert's men, had been buried in very shallow graves—probably in one common grave—" That the dead bodies of our murthered neighbours buried out of the towne shall be better covered betwixt this and February 2 next, for the effecting hereof we order that the two bailiffs or any other officer giving notice or warning to any house, it shall send one thither, with a spade or a whisket for the covering of them as aforesaid." Parliament in this same year granted twenty pounds for the widows and orphans of those who had been slain, and the town was authorised to take five hundred tons of timber from the woods of the neighbouring Royalist gentry to repair the houses ruined in the sieges, as well as lead from the ruins of Lathom House.

PRINCE RUPERT'S QUARTERS DURING HIS SIEGE OF LIVERPOOL

67

AN AMUSING MISTAKE

ON the occasion of the Coronation of George IV. the Corporation of Liverpool had taken an active part in arranging festivities in the town in honour of the event, and had subscribed £500 to the expenses. But, ten years later, when William IV. and Queen Adelaide were crowned, the body made no suggestion for the town celebrating the day, and appeared to take no interest whatever in the matter. A meeting was therefore called at which a resolution was passed, "that it is a duty which the inhabitants owe to their king and country to express their joy at the coronation of His Majesty and his royal consort." A deputation was also appointed to wait upon the Mayor requesting him to call a meeting to consult the inhabitants as to the best way of expressing their loyalty. Accordingly the deputation waited upon the Mayor, but he declined to call a town's meeting on the ground that "the deputation presented something of a party appearance, and that he could not lend himself to party objects." He suggested that it would be better for the deputation to prepare a requisition. This was done, and within a few hours a requisition for a meeting, signed by nearly one hundred men of standing in Liverpool, was laid before him. To this he made answer, " As I see the requisition does not embrace a decided union of all parties, I must respectfully beg to decline complying with the request."

Feeling was running very high in Liverpool at that time on the question of Parliamentary Reform, and most of the deputation were Reformers. The Mayor's answer was received with open disapprobation and a public open-air meeting was held in Clayton Square, at which resolu-tions were passed condemning the Mayor's conduct and appointing a public procession to take place on the following day—that of the coronation. The procession duly took place ; it consisted chiefly of the Trades and Friendly Societies—and at its close another open-air meeting was held at which addresses were voted to the King and Queen.

Although the Mayor and the Town Council declined to take any public notice of the coronation, they voted " loyal and dutiful " addresses to King William and Queen Adelaide. These were confided for presentation in London to the Mayor, Mr. Thomas Brancker, who was accompanied by Alderman Bourne and Sir George Drinkwater. The address from the town-meeting was given into the charge of Mr. John Ewart. These addresses were presented to King William at St. James's Palace on September 13, at a *levée*, and in consequence of there being two addresses from Liverpool, in place of one, an amusing mistake very nearly became an actual fact.

Mr. Ewart, with the town's address, was first. As he knelt to present the address the King, taking the royal sword from an attendant, was about to give him the accolade, thinking he was the Mayor of Liverpool. Mr. Ewart, seeing the sword descending upon his shoulder, called out, " Not me. Don't knight me."

" Why, which is the Mayor of Liverpool ? " the King asked, not at all pleased.

His Majesty was then informed that the Mayor of Liverpool was behind, and amidst the amusement of the King and the whole Court the Mayor and the Bailiffs were introduced by Lord Melbourne. This time there was no protest against knighthood, and the Mayor rose from his knees Sir Thomas Brancker.

A ROYAL "SCENE" AT LIVERPOOL

A CURIOUS example of the bad manners of George IV. is given by the Rev. James Aspinall. In 1803, Prince William, afterwards Duke of Gloucester, the nephew of George III., was appointed Commander of the Forces in the Liverpool district, and took up his residence at San Domingo House, Everton. Three years later the Prince of Wales (afterwards George IV.) and the Duke of Clarence (afterwards William IV.) were the guests of the Earl of Derby at Knowsley, and during that time visited Liverpool, where they were rapturously and enthusiastically received.

The new Exchange Buildings were being built at that time, and the two brothers were driven in a coach round the arcades, a thing that has never been done before or since. The relations between the three royal highnesses were not of the most cordial character, Prince William of Gloucester being of a very different type from either the Prince of Wales or the Duke of Clarence. It was characteristic of George IV. that he should make that difference an occasion for insult.

" A magnificent banquet was given at the Town Hall by the Mayor, Mr. Henry Clay. The Prince of Wales, the Duke of Clarence, Prince William of Gloucester, the Earls of Derby and Sefton, with a crowd of military officers, were present. After dinner the usual toasts were proposed—then the ' Prince of Wales ' and the ' Duke of Clarence,' each with three times three. At last it was the Prince's turn, when, under the influence of some demon of mischief, the Mayor, instead of proposing his health as usual with all his titles and with all the honours, foolishly consulted the Prince of Wales and the Duke of Clarence on the subject, asking in what form he should give the toast, and whether he should say ' Highness ' or ' Royal Highness.' The answer of the Prince of Wales was said to be, ' Certainly

not " Royal Highness," and without the honours ; ' while the Duke of Clarence more plainly replied, ' D—n him, don't give him at all.' The Mayor then rose and simply proposed, ' The Commander-in-Chief of the District, Prince William Frederick of Gloucester.' It was drunk in solemn silence. The company looked grave, feeling that a gross insult had been offered to the late god of Liverpool's adoration. Fierce glances were exchanged between the staff officers and the other military men present. The Prince himself writhed under the stroke like a wounded tiger smarting under the lash of the slander: fire and brimstone, and the devil himself flashed from his eyes, but he kept his seat. Presently the fearful and appalling silence was broken by the Mayor calling out as the next toast, ' The Lord Lieutenant of the County, with three times three '; the *three times three* omitted at the name of the Commander-in-Chief being revived with that of the next toast. A thunderbolt falling into the midst of the party could not have caused more astonishment and excitement. There could be no mistake now. The insult was meant to be an insult, and nothing but an open, prominent, and most insulting insult. The words had hardly passed from the lips of the Mayor, when Prince William, glancing a signal to his Staff who had their eyes fixed on him, rose from his seat and left the room, followed not only by them, but by the whole of the military officers of his command who were present, leaving the table almost deserted, the Mayor gaping in amazement, and the royal cousins astounded at the spirit which they had evoked, more perhaps in mischief than in wanton insolence."

If Mr. Aspinall had left out the words " more perhaps in mischief," the remaining " wanton insolence " would have accurately described the intention of the royal brothers.

GENERAL SIR BANASTRE TARLETON

ONE of the most distinguished Lancashire soldiers during the eighteenth century was Banastre Tarleton, the son of a Liverpool merchant. He was born in 1754, at his father's house in Water Street, then the favourite place of residence for the higher classes of the town. The Tarletons had been for many generations one of the most influential families in Liverpool. Originally the family was settled at Aigburth. In the seventeenth and early in the eighteenth century, when communication between London and Liverpool was both difficult and tedious, many of the landed gentry possessed houses in Liverpool, and through some branch of their family were connected with trade, as for example the Norrises of Speke, the Claytons of Fulwood, the Blackburnes of Hale, the Banastres of Bank, and the Tarletons.

Banastre Tarleton was educated with a view to becoming a barrister, but after being entered in one of the Inns of Court, having previously been to Oxford, he went into the Army, a commission as Cornet in the King's Dragoon Guards being purchased for him. In those days before competitive examinations, commissions in the Army were bought. The war between England and her American colonies had broken out about this time, and young Tarleton obtained leave to accompany Lord Cornwallis, who was taking out reinforcements, as a volunteer.

He proved himself a most dashing soldier, one of his earliest exploits being the capture of the American General Lee. By the time he was twenty-three he had been promoted to be a brigade-major of cavalry, and in the following year was appointed lieutenant-colonel commandant of the British Legion—a force of mixed

infantry and cavalry which had been known as the Caledonian Volunteers, but which after the young colonel's appointment was called Tarleton's Green Horse, from the colour of the facings upon the uniform. On one occasion Tarleton, by a most skilful movement of his irregular force, surprised three regiments of the enemy's cavalry, and after destroying them, captured all their stores and baggage, as well as four hundred horses. But his most brilliant exploit was when he was sent to break up the Virginian General Assembly. He only had two hundred and fifty men, cavalry and mounted infantry; but such was his expedition that he entirely surprised the Assembly. Destroying twelve wagons laden with arms and clothing on the way, he dashed into the village of Charlottenville where the Assembly was sitting, by crossing a ford through a river, and after dispersing the guard on the opposite bank seized seven members of the Assembly as well as an enormous store of firearms, gunpowder, tobacco, clothing and stores. He was rewarded with promotion to the rank of lieutenant-colonel in the Army, being then twenty-seven.

But in this same year (1781) Lord Cornwallis was shut up by Washington in Yorktown, Tarleton being also shut in at Gloucester, which he commanded with only six hundred men. Cornwallis was obliged to capitulate after vainly waiting for the relief which came too late, and on October 19, 1781, Yorktown and Gloucester were surrendered. Tarleton thus became a prisoner of war. He was released on parole early in the following year, and returned to England.

The bravery and dashing exploits of the young soldier stood out in bold relief against the dilatoriness and inefficiency of some of the leaders in that deplorable war; and when he arrived in England Tarleton found himself a popular hero, especially in his native Liverpool, where he was received with wild enthusiasm.

Having achieved this brilliant military reputation, Tarleton now had the ambition to enter Parliament, and in 1784 offered himself as a candidate for Liverpool, where his gallant bearing, his frank and easy manners, had made him extremely popular " especially with the shipwrights and market women," says one who had more respect for the Colonel as a soldier than as a politician. In this first contest, distinguished military service and popular manners did not gain Tarleton a seat, his place being third on the list. But six years later there was another election. The two sitting members, Bamber Gascoyne and Lord Penrhyn, put forward their manifestoes, as did also Tarleton, but finding that a coalition had taken place between the friends and supporters of the two old members, he saw no chance of success. He therefore proposed to withdraw; when an economy proved fatal to the other side.

During election times beer flowed copiously and freely for the " free and independent electors " at the expense of the candidates. The arrangement between the Gascoyne party and the Penrhyn party settled the election, and there being no necessity to influence the electors either on one side or the other, the flow of free beer was cut off. Many were the grumblings and great the discontent in consequence. A friend of Colonel Tarleton seized upon this discontent with great adroitness. Bringing a barrel of ale into a street near the Exchange, he knocked out the head, and began distributing the contents to the crowd which quickly gathered, at the same time holding forth on the injustice of the coalition, and the duty of the people to support their military hero. The suggestion, supported as it was by unlimited ale, quickly spread, and an address was presented to Tarleton begging him to come forward. The mayor, and the bailiffs of the merchants and the tradesmen, called a meeting " to settle the question with as little interruption as possible to the trade of the town," but it broke up in confusion. A bitter contest followed, extending over seven days. During the first two days the polling for the three candidates was nearly equal, but the freemen, who had been exasperated against the self-elected Common Council, —another grievance cleverly made use of by the Tarleton party,—then voted solidly for the Colonel. At the close of the poll the numbers stood, Tarleton 1269; Gascoyne 888; Penrhyn 716.

The action of the Common Council in excluding the burgesses from all share in local affairs certainly turned the scale in Tarleton's favour. In one of the manifestoes issued by his party, Mr. John Foster, a member of a family who during several generations managed the architectural and building affairs of the Corporation, is thus described : " Consider the insult offered you by the Body Corporate in bestowing all the work on young F——r, a fellow of yesterday ; an upstart, whose arrogance, impudence and ignorance are only surpassed by the blunders he commits hourly in his profession." The same feeling was voiced in the following doggrel, which was called " The Colonel's Ballad." The rhymes are curious :—

" Freeman, where is your boasted magnanimity ?
Where's your boasted courage flown ?
Quite perverted by pusillanimity,
    Scarce can call your souls your own.

What your colonel has won so victoriously,
  Crowned with conquest in the field,
You have relinquished, and O most in-
    gloriously
  To oppression tamely yield.

Freedom now for her flight makes prepara-
    tive,
  See her weeping quit the shore !
Freemen's loss is past all comparative,
  Never to behold her more !

Great God, arise : and with fate now *exorgi-
    tale,*
  Strike with thy vindictive frown,
Make oppressors their plunder *egorgilale,*
  And relieve a weeping town."

It was a noticeable fact that none of
the addresses of the candidates at this
election contained any reference to politics,
each one basing his claims upon his
attentions to the interests of the borough.
Six years later this was changed. All
the time Tarleton had been in Parliament he had taken the Whig or Opposition side, and the Liverpool Tories,
therefore, did their best to oust him from
the seat, bringing in his own brother,
John Tarleton, to oppose him. Feeling
ran to great heights, and Colonel Bryan
Blundell, another distinguished Liverpool
soldier, who had intended to offer himself
as a candidate, wrote : " On my arrival
in my native town I found it engaged in
so extraordinary a contest, so much confusion the consequence, I must confess my
own feelings will not allow me to add to
it by making an offer of my humble
services." The majority of the Liverpool
people were on the side of the Government, that is, Tory ; but just as the
cutting off of free beer gained him his
first election, the interposition of his
brother gained Tarleton his second.
This ungenerous opposition roused strong
indignation, which was expressed in the
following squib :—

" *Liverpool, May* 28, 1796.

" Lost this morning about nine
o'clock, that very small portion of
popularity which I have lately acquired
by abusing and misrepresenting my
brother, his family and friends. Who-
ever will bring any part of it to my
committee-room in Brunswick Street
shall receive a handsome reward from my
arch-treasurer, J——n B——n,[1] Esq.,
who, knowing my very extraordinary
manœuvring abilities, has wisely accepted a sufficient security from me to
indemnify himself and other friends.
                      " J—— T——."[2]

The Tories on their side were no less
bitter, and Banastre Tarleton's name was
now openly coupled with that of the
beautiful but frail " Perdita," to whom
George IV., as Prince of Wales, was
Florizel ; every capital was made of a
circumstance which certainly did not
redound to the credit of Tarleton, now
become a general. But his supporters
answered with the following song, to the
tune of " O ! dear, what can the matter
be ? " :

"TARLETON AND LIBERTY.

" From a cruise of six years for the good of
    the nation,
In which our commander ne'er fled from his
    station,
But battled with many a royal oration,
    Our brave man of war has come home.
    Huzza, Tarleton and Liberty
          Tarleton and Liberty.
    Liverpool welcomes him home.

When taxes and war menaced danger
    around him,
And placemen and courtiers endeavour'd to
    sound him,
A true British patriot we ever have found
    him,
    As such let us welcome him home.
          Huzza, etc.

[1] John Bolton, a prominent Liverpool Tory.
[2] John Tarleton.

72

When credit and property call'd for his aid, sirs,
He fought for our rights and protected our trade, sirs,
Which enemies vainly may try to invade, sirs,
While patriots flourish at home.
Huzza, etc.

Like a rock in the midst of the wide stormy ocean,
He stood grim and free 'midst the threaten'd commotion,
And scorned from our foes to solicit promotion,
Our hearts were his pride and his home.
Huzza, etc.

With freedom and truth, and an Englishman's spirit,
He knows that the proudest distinction is merit,
Then let him from us the rich title inherit,
And Liverpool still be his home.
Huzza, etc."

Tarleton was returned again for Liverpool in 1802, at an election which was marked by bitter party feeling and a serious riot. A number of men, principally sailors, sacked several houses in a street near the old dock. The tenant of one of these houses defended his home vigorously, shooting one of the rioters dead, and wounding another. This so infuriated the mob that they broke down the door, and haling the man out of his house, beat him to death.

Four years later there was another election, at which Tarleton came out at the bottom of the poll, William Roscoe being at the head. But Tarleton's retirement was only a brief one, for the following year the Government resigned upon George III.'s bitter opposition to a bill to relax the penal laws still existing against Roman Catholics, to the extent of permitting them to act as officers in the army and navy without taking the oaths of abjuration and supremacy. The

elections that ensued were memorable for the religious bitterness and virulence displayed; all over the country they were fought under the cry of " No Popery." But nowhere was the election fought with such rancour and animosity as at Liverpool. In addition to the religious question, Liverpool had a special grievance of its own against the late Government, and especially against their late member, William Roscoe. This grievance was the abolition of the slave trade on March 25, 1807, a measure for which Roscoe had voted.

General Tarleton was begged to stand again for Liverpool; Roscoe's friends applied to him to stand also, but the terrible riot and bloodshed which attended his entry into the town on May 2, 1807, caused him to withdraw. The procession arranged in his honour was fallen upon by men with green favours (Tarleton's colour), and a large number of the seamen who had been discharged from the vessels formerly engaged in the slave trade. The same night there was a fierce fight between the rival parties, in which one of Roscoe's supporters was killed and many were wounded. Never had such scenes been witnessed at a Liverpool election before, and Roscoe, utterly disgusted, withdrew his candidature, saying, " If the representation of Liverpool can only be obtained by violence and bloodshed, I leave the honour of it to those who choose to contend for it."

During the six days that the election lasted, fighting and brawling were of constant occurrence, each side also vying with the other in the scurrility, coarseness, and venom of their squibs and broadsheets.

In the campaign in America, Tarleton had lost two of the fingers of one of his hands, and on the hustings at election

times, when hardly pressed by his opponents, he would hold up his wounded
hand, making great capital of this evidence of his services to his country, and
greatly impressing the easily-swayed mob.
This trick is alluded to in one of the

O ! my poor wounded hand and all my fine
  clack, sirs,
Will serve no more Obi [1] or Three-finger'd
  Jack, sirs ;
For Roscoe and freedom they shout, 'tis a
  fact, sirs ;
Alas ! I shall never more say *aye* or *no.*"

SIR BANASTRE TARLETON
(After Sir Joshua Reynolds)
(By permission of Messrs. Methuen)

squibs published during this bitterly-
fought election of 1806—

" My three-finger'd hand I keep constantly
  showing,
But the once blind electors are all grown
  too knowing,
Of Roscoe and freedom they're constantly
  crowing ;
O ! I shall never more say *aye* or *no*,

Nevertheless, Tarleton was returned at
the head of the poll with 1461 votes, and
Roscoe, whose friends had carried on the
contest in spite of his withdrawal, at the
bottom, with 379.

Thus, for a further six years, Tarleton
represented his native place, but at the

[1] This is a reference to the slave trade which
Tarleton had supported.

74

following election of 1812, so low had he fallen in his townsmen's favour that it was with difficulty he could find a person to nominate him, and he only polled eleven votes.

The popular idol of 1790, and the member for Liverpool for twenty-two years, with the exception of the brief interval when Roscoe represented the town, was received now with only the most open and undisguised indifference. Great changes had taken place during those twenty-two years. The French Revolution had entirely altered the nature and the aims of English politics; Liverpool, too, under the influence of men like William Roscoe and her increasing trade, had changed also. But Tarleton had not changed, and here was the cause of Liverpool's indifference to her former hero. "As a speaker in the House of Commons he evinced earnestness and some power," it has been said of him, "but his ignorance of mercantile matters and love of pleasure made him no very efficient representative of an important commercial town like Liverpool."

After this election Tarleton had no further connection with Liverpool. In 1817 he was created a baronet, and died sixteen years later in Shropshire in his eightieth year.

Tarleton was a great figure in the social world in London, and his portrait by Sir Joshua Reynolds is one of the best male portraits by that great artist. The prints of this picture—from one of which the illustration is taken—had one of the largest sales of the prints of any of Sir Joshua's paintings.

LIVERPOOL 1889

THE STORY OF LIVERPOOL'S
WATER SUPPLY

THE history of Liverpool's water-supply as a record of wrangling, opposition, and counter-opposition during nearly a hundred years has no equal in any other city in the kingdom. Originally the town was supplied by wells, sunk at only a moderate distance in the new red sandstone; but as these collected only surface water from the rock, or were fed by small springs, they gradually became exhausted as the houses and population increased under the rising prosperity of the port. As early as 1709 the water question seems to have caused some apprehension to the Corporation, for in that year Sir Cleave Moore obtained an Act of Parliament enabling the Corporation to make a grant to Sir Cleave Moore to bring water into Liverpool from Bootle Springs. Of the many springs welling up from the outcrop of the new red sandstone, those at Bootle were the most abundant, providing sufficient water to turn a mill after issuing from the earth. But before advantage could be taken of the Act, Sir Cleave Moore's estates were sold to the then Earl of Derby, and for nearly a century the Act remained a dead letter.

The next scheme was to bring water from the Moss Lake, and for nearly twenty years this seems to have been satisfactory. A company was formed, the shares being ten pounds apiece, and a reservoir was built near the site of the Gallows Mills in London Road to which the water from the lake was carried in an open trench or conduit, and until 1742 all went well. But in that year, after continuous heavy rain, the reservoir burst its banks and the town was flooded, the water rising to the second floor of the houses in Lord Street, and as high as the gallery of the old almshouses at the bottom of Dale Street. At the same time there was an unusually high tide, and the water overran the quays of the Old Dock.

Liverpool on that unfortunate day had a great deal more water than her people cared for. The bursting of the reservoir appears to have had a discouraging effect upon the company and the townspeople for we hear no more of the supply from the Moss Lake, but in its stead constant references to scarcity of water. Indeed, water became a valuable commodity in Liverpool, and such advertisements as the following were common in the newspapers:—

"At Edmund Parker's pump on Shaw's Brow, may be had water at 9d. per butt, for watering shipping and sugar-houses; and is as soft for washing and boiling peese &c., as any in the town. Any merchant or captain of a ship &c., sending to his house, next to Mr. Chaffer's china pothouse, may be served immediately by their humble servant, Edmund Parker."

This appeared on November 17, 1758. In the following August the possession of a well was clearly the chief value of the houses in the following advertisement:—
"To be sold, to the highest bidder, two dwelling-houses at Bevington Bush, with a well of good water that will supply five or six carts, and a gin pump &c."

So matters went on until 1764, water gradually becoming so scarce that it was doled out by women, who went about the town with water-carts, at so much a "heshin," or bucket. Then the idea of utilizing the Bootle Springs was revived, and in 1765 a jury was summoned to sit at the Everton coffee-house on behalf of John Jordan, to whom Sir Cleave Moore's rights had been assigned, to consider what damage would be inflicted upon several landowners by the conduit, which it was proposed should be made between Bootle and Liverpool, to bring the Bootle water into the town. The suggestion met with a determined and bitter opposition. A pamphlet was issued addressed "To the Landowners and Inhabitants of Liverpool," with the title, "Reasons why Mr. Jordan should not be permitted to prosecute his scheme of bringing water from Bootle Springs." Some of the reasons brought forward have a curious childishness to-day. "The present mode of supply is so very convenient, expeditious and reasonable (four pailfuls being sold for one penny), and so many poor families getting their bread by it, and there being one general town's well, to which many families resort, it is cheap or cheaper than by the method Mr. Jordan proposes," was brought forward, despite the fact of the daily inconvenience to the inhabitants of being obliged to buy water by the pailful. Another reason was, "Really the water of Bootle springs is a poor, thin water, very unfit for brewing or many other purposes. An eminent Brewer very emphatically styles it only half water; whereas the town's springs have been found upon trial to be lighter than any of the springs at a distance."

Other "reasons" against the scheme were the breaking up of the streets for the laying of pipes, that the selfsame pipes passing under land used for brickfields would reduce its value from five hundred pounds to fifty pounds an acre; and that many poor people who carried water in the town would lose their employment.

This pamphlet roused a successful opposition, from which Liverpool reaped the bitter and expensive fruit in the next century.

By the Improvement Act of 1786 the Corporation was empowered to supply the town with water from the local springs, but no action was taken, and matters remained precisely in the same state, notwithstanding the steady expansion of the town, until 1799, when an Act of Parliament was obtained to revise the Bootle scheme, and a company was formed to carry the Act into effect. Instantly the Corporation took alarm, and issued a proposal to supply the town with water from what were called "the town springs." Another company was formed, the shares being two hundred pounds each, every one of which was taken up a few hours after their issue. The Corporation transferred all its rights and powers to this company, on the stipulation of a share in the profits. But there never were any profits.

Liverpool now had two rival water companies, and both went vigorously to work. Streets were torn up and pipes laid along them—these pipes were elm trees bored through the centre. Wells were sunk, pumping engines erected; all the paraphernalia for supplying water to an already large and growing town was duplicated. The Corporation company utilized the natural springs oozing from the hill-side and built pumping-stations in Hotham Street, and afterwards in Berry Street. The Bootle company established their reservoir and pumping-station in the Pump Fields, near the Vauxhall Road. Each year the demands of the town increased, and each year both companies made increased efforts to meet the demands, but in 1845, when a sanitary system began to be generally installed in the houses, they could not produce the necessary supply. The quantity of water had risen from ten gallons per head a day to twenty gallons. Confronted by this failure both the Corporation and the townspeople were of one mind. They determined to strike against the monopoly of the two companies and make the water supply a public concern. Their opportunity came in 1846, when the two companies applied to Parliament for an extension of their powers. Opposition to this extension was decided upon, but before this could be undertaken an alternative scheme to that proposed by the companies had to be laid before Parliament. Here, the history of Bootle strengthened in their opinion by the results of a deep well being sunk in Green Lane, West Derby, by the Highway Board. The Corporation favoured the Rivington Pike scheme. There were furious local discussions, which were echoed in London when the matter of Liverpool's water had to be decided by Parliament, but with this difference—in Liverpool it was a matter of words, in London it was a matter of enormous

RIVINGTON PIKE

water *versus* water from the sandstone rock of the preceding century repeated itself. Three schemes were brought forward. One was that water should be brought from Bala Lake, another that water should be collected in the Rivington Pike district and brought to Liverpool; and the third, that if the red sandstone at home were properly developed it would yield an ample return. Three parties at once sprang into existence, each eagerly advocating the advantages of its favoured plan. The Rivington Pike scheme and the scheme of local supply had the larger number of supporters, the latter being expense. The Rivington Pike scheme received the assent of Parliament, with the rider that the two water companies must be compensated, a compensation that amounted to over half a million of money. So, what with this compensation and the expenses of the parliamentary inquiry, Liverpool had a pretty bill to pay.

The town was divided into two factions, Pikists and Anti-Pikists; and the Pikists having carried the Bill were anxious for the work to begin at once. But the Anti-Pikists, who had a large following, anxious that the local possibilities should be fully tested before the further large expenditure was started upon, clamoured for delay. The Pikists had a majority on the Town Council, and tenders were invited for the work, every effort being made to push the work forward. This drove the Anti-Pikists to further action. Committees were formed, pamphlets written and scattered broad-cast, public meetings were held, meetings that were the scenes of wild disorder and bitter attack upon the Council; and above all the *Liverpool Mercury* poured all its thunder and its sarcasm upon the Rivington Pike scheme and its supporters. The newspaper was the Anti-Pikists' most useful ally, but in the height of the discussion its business affairs became involved, and it was sold. Under the new ownership the paper became a " preacher of the faith it had once laboured to destroy"; and its valuable support was given to the other side. Nothing daunted, the Anti-Pikists still fought and agitated, and in 1850 they succeeded in getting a majority on the Town Council. Great was the jubilation, and loud were their taunts and triumph. But a bitter awakening came to them. On the day before the borough

elections, which had given them the majority, had taken place, the contract for the construction of the main portion of the works had been sealed with the seal of the Corporation. Their victory had come too late, yet they did not yield to defeat without a further struggle. They suspended the works and instituted a court of inquiry, agreeing to abide by the decision of the referee, one of the foremost' civil engineers in the country. The inquiry was long, the evidence produced on both sides was most exhaustive ; and when the referee's report was sent in to the Anti-Pikist Town Council it recommended the carrying out of the Rivington Pike scheme !

This was the hardest blow the Anti-Pikists had suffered, but true to their undertaking they accepted the decision, and the work was carried out. Writing in 1875, Mr. J. A. Picton says: " With subsequent additions and purchase of compensation waters the supply to the town, notwithstanding the great increase of population, has never failed in seasons of the greatest drought." To-day, as we know, Liverpool has been forced to go farther afield for her water-supply.

THE NEAREST SEA=FIGHT TO LANCASHIRE

IN our continuous wars with the French there were very few occasions in which naval engagements took place in home waters, and fewer still when they were fought off the northern coasts. Only once did the French war vessels approach the Lancashire shore. This was in 1760, when Admiral Thurot was defeated by Captain Elliot and his whole squadron of five frigates captured and taken in triumph into Ramsey Bay.

Thurot had a curious history. He began life as a smuggler, became a pirate, and ended as a French admiral of renown. When only fifteen years old he left Dunkirk with an Irish smuggler named Farrell, and settled in the Isle of Man, which was then a veritable Tom Tiddler's ground for smugglers. In those days the English laws did not extend to the island. " His Majesty of Great Britain," said a King's Commission, " is master of the seas, yet the Isle of Man has jurisdiction of so much round the island that a master of a ship has no more to do than catch his opportunity of coming within the piles where he is secure from any danger from the King's officers." Smuggling, in consequence, was an openly followed occupation, and Thurot, entering the service of a Manx runner of contraband as a sailor, speedily gained a knowledge of seamanship, which laid the foundation of his later exploits. The vessel upon which he served chiefly ran from the Isle of Man to Anglesey, and it required no little daring and dexterity to avoid the revenue cutters which patrolled those waters. Little wonder, therefore, that after ten years of such experience Thurot became not only a most practised smuggler, but also a daring and brilliant sailor. When he was twenty-five he went to live at Boulogne, where he speedily became one of the leaders of the band of smugglers settled there. War broke out with England in 1755, and Thurot immediately joined the privateers of Dunkirk, which worked terrible havoc upon British merchantmen. His exploits in this direction attracted the attention of the French Government. He was given the command of a frigate in the Navy, and such was his success that two years later he was made an Admiral and given the command of a small squadron.

The French at this time were contemplating the invasion of England. Attacks upon the unprotected Irish coast, they thought, would distract the attention of the English Government, whilst the sending of troops to repel a French landing in Ireland would weaken the defences of England and so facilitate the invasion. A man of daring and of expert seamanship was needed for the task, and the choice therefore fell upon Thurot, who late in 1759 left Dunkirk harbour with a squadron of five ships and one thousand seven hundred men. He was given a roving commission, to attack where he chose, and where he deemed most harm could be done.

The alarm in Liverpool upon the receipt of these tidings was intense; and the following account of the hasty preparations made in the town appeared in Williamson's *Advertiser* of November 9, 1759 : " On Sunday evening the account of a French squadron being sailed from Dunkirk, destined for the north channel, arrived here; upon which Lawrence Spencer, Esqre., Mayor, convened the gentlemen merchants at the Exchange, to consider putting the town immediately into a proper state of defence against any sudden attempt of the enemy, when it was unanimously resolved to enter into an association and subscription for defending the town in the best manner, and a committee of gentlemen was appointed to manage the whole. Expresses were that night despatched to His Majesty praying for a commission to be granted to the Mayor in the same manner as was done in the year 1745, and as soon as the commission comes down it is proposed to raise 20 companies of 100 men each. At the request of the committee a return of the muskets in the hands of the merchants and dealers has been made, and it is found that on an emergency upwards of 4,000 men may be completed armed, exclusive of the arms in private persons' hands ; and it is expected that the gentlemen of the field and saddle will form themselves into squadrons of light horse, being at least 500 strong. Pilot boats have been sent out and properly stationed, to give the earliest intelligence in case of the enemy's steering this course, and regular measures concerted to destroy on their approach all the buoys, and blow up the land-marks leading into the harbour. To-morrow, Saturday, November 10th, the anniversary of the birth of our most gracious Sovereign George II., the five new batteries will be opened, and a Royal salute given on the occasion. They are deemed the completest of the kind in England, and were erected at the expense of the gentlemen merchants and tradesmen, who voluntarily opened a subscription for that purpose; and consist of two *batteries d'enfilade* scouring the whole river ; a *battery en charpe*, which plays obliquely ; a *battery per camerade*, so contrived as to fire at the same time upon one body ; and a battery in form zig-zag, making several angles, completely sheltering the garrison from being enfiladed or fired on in a straight line. This week upwards of seventy heavy guns have been mounted on the platforms, and several hundred men employed in mounting them."

Liverpool was thus well protected against any sudden attack by Admiral Thurot, who for some time continued his depredations with impunity. After scouring the Irish Channel and "picking up a great many of our merchantmen," he lost, through bad weather, two of his ships and half his men. But in no wise daunted, he put into the Island of Islay about the middle of February 1760, where he commandeered provisions and stores.

Sailing from Islay into Belfast Lough he landed a number of men at Carrickfergus, and proceeded to loot the town before the astonished inhabitants had realized the enemy had suddenly descended upon them. Recovering from their surprise, however, they made such a determined attack upon the French sailors that the latter were compelled to withdraw to their boats, and a little while afterwards the French squadron was racing out to sea. A doggerel ballad was composed upon the failure to capture Carrickfergus :—

" Thurot jumped out of his hammock, and
    unto his men did say,
' Come, strike your colours low, boys, they'll
    sink us in the sea ;
Come, weigh your anchors, ho, boys, make
    all the haste you can ;
We'll steer sou' and sou' east, bound for
    the Isle of Man.' "

There were several other verses in the same strain, the conclusion being :—

" Now to conclude and finish, and for to
    end my lay,
May the Irish beat the French on land
    and the English them by sea."

News of the attack speedily reached Captain Elliot, who had command of three frigates at Kinsale. He instantly set out in search of the bold French Admiral, and rounding the Mull of Galloway on the 28th February saw his squadron lying at anchor near the

−H

entrance to the Bay of Luce. Elliot at once manœuvred to drive the French war vessels into the bay, but, observing this, Thurot weighed anchor and stood out to sea in the direction of the Isle of Man. Elliot followed in hot pursuit and a terrific battle took place, being maintained on both sides for an hour and a half with great spirit and determination, when the French struck their colours. The whole squadron was taken by Elliot into Ramsey Bay.

The Scottish historian Train, was staying in the Isle of Man at the time, and thus described the scene on one of the captured ships, the *Belleisle :* " On hearing of Thurot being brought into Ramsey Bay on Thursday last I went there to see the ships. On getting aboard the *Belleisle* I was struck with astonishment! Turn which way I would, nothing but scattered limbs and dead and dying men met my view. The decks and sides of the ships could only be compared to a slaughter house, there being nearly two hundred men killed on board the *Belleisle* besides what the other ships lost. The French must have plundered all before them at Carrickfergus, for I saw one of them stripped which had eight women's shifts on him. They had plenty of children's clothes, shoes, caps, ruffles, buttons, thimbles and pins, with a store of grey yarn. The English seamen looked upon the French as a parcel of poltroons by their behaviour."

Thurot himself was killed early in the action, and it was generally believed that his body was thrown overboard. This was the case, but it was first sewn in a silk velvet carpet. The nearest point of the mainland is Mochrum in Galloway, and here, after the action, every tide, it was said, washed bodies of French sailors ashore. Amongst these was the body of Thurot. When the carpet was taken off he was found to be wearing the full dress uniform of a French admiral, and if further identification had been needed, it was given by the marks on his linen and a silver tobacco-box upon which his name was engraved in full.

The remains were buried by order of Sir William Maxwell of Monteith, the Lord of the Manor, in the cemetery of Mochrum. Sir William attended the funeral as chief mourner. The carpet in which Thurot's body was sewn was kept for a long time at Monteith House ; the tobacco-box was presented to the victorious Captain Elliot. Thurot was described as being about thirty years of age, of short stature but well made, having bright black eyes and a fresh complexion, and of a " frank, humane and affable disposition."

Never before nor since had a foreign foe approached so near to Lancashire ; and it was a strange coincidence that Thurot should meet his death while fighting for his country in the very locality in which he learned to be a sailor.

THE DRAINING OF MARTIN MERE

A S late as the end of the seventeenth century there was a large lake called Martin Mere, some two miles from Southport. Several attempts were made to drain the Mere and reclaim the land, with varying success and failure, until Mr. Thomas Eccleston of Scarisbrick Hall, a noted agriculturist of his time, took up the matter in 1781. He received the gold medal of the Society of Arts, Manufactures and Commerce, in reward, and the following is the account of his labours which he communicated to the society, and which was published in the seventh volume of their "Transactions," in 1786.

"Martin-Meer," wrote Mr. Eccleston, "was formerly a large pool, or lake of fresh water of an irregular form, surrounded chiefly by mosses and boggy land, containing near one thousand seven hundred and seventeen acres, of eight yards to the pole, which is the customary measure of the neighbourhood (about three thousand six hundred and thirty-two statute acres). It lies in the different manors of Scarisbrick, Burscough, North Meols, Tarleton and Rufford.

"About the year 1692, Mr. Fleetwood of Bank Hall proposed to the several other proprietors to drain Martin-Meer on condition that a lease (for the whole) for three lives and thirty-one years should be granted him, which they agreed to; and Mr. Fleetwood obtained an act of parliament the same year to empower him to effect it. The following year he began the work : his plan was, to discharge the waters immediately into the sea, at the mouth of the River Ribble, which before had forced themselves a passage into the River Douglas, when the Meer waters were raised above their usual height by land floods. . . . The

intermediate ground between Martin-Meer and the Douglas lying considerably higher than the Meer, occasioned the stagnation, and kept it continuously full.

"Mr. Fleetwood began the undertaking by making a canal, or sluice twenty-four feet wide, of a depth sufficiently lower than the Meer, which he cut from the Ribble mouth through an embanked saltmarsh, and then through a moss or bog in North Meols, about a mile and a half in length ; and he continued it through the lowest part of the Meer. To prevent the sea from rushing up the canal, and overflowing the Meer, which lies ten feet lower than high-water mark at the spring-tides, he erected in his canal, near the sea, a pair of flood-gates, which shut when the sea waters rose higher than those in the canal, and opened again by the sluice stream when the sea retired. In this place, the mouth of the Ribble is nearly five miles over at the spring tides ; but the bend of the river at low water is no more than a furlong in breadth, and it lies under the Lythem, or opposite shore to the flood-gates, about the distance of four miles from them. This is a very unfavourable circumstance to the draining of the Meer, as it greatly diminishes the effect of the out-fall by the length of the way the waters have to run over a very flat, loose, flying sandy coast, before they can disembogue into the river. These sands in a few years after the drainage was finished, drifting by the winds into the out-fall sluice soon obstructed the flow of the waters, and in a short time choked up the passage, which had been made sufficiently deep to carry them off.

"The spring tides in boisterous weather brought up great quantities of mud to the flood-gates ; here it lodged in sediment for want of a powerful current in dry seasons to wash it away; thus the wished for effect of so much labour was frustrated, for the Meer was once more nearly reduced to its primitive state. In order to remove the destructive obstacle of mud and sand, the managers for Mr. Fleetwood, in the year 1714, thought it most advisable to raise the sill or threshold of the flood-gates, which they elevated twenty inches: this, with some other measures then adopted, did, for some time enable them to keep the flood-gates free from the above-mentioned obstructions. But it proved very detrimental, for so much fall was lost, that the arable and meadow grounds upon the Meer diminished greatly in value by the water remaining upon them all the winter, and very late oftentimes in the spring season. By a gradual, continual loss of out-fall amongst the sands, and by the sluice on the marsh and other parts wrecking up, the Meer lands for many years were only made use of as a poor, fenny, watery pasture for the cattle of the neighbourhood, and that for a part of the summer months only.

"Some time afterwards, Mr. Fleetwood's executors continued their sluice farther upon the shore, and erected a new pair of flood-gates, winged with stone walls, considerably nearer to the out-fall, and they found great benefit from it, as the gates were much less liable to be obstructed by the sand and mud brought up by the tide.

"About the year 1750 Mr. Fleetwood's lease expired, and in 1755 the flood-gates were washed down by a very uncommon high tide, but were rebuilt (fourteen feet wide) at the joint expense of the proprietors, in whose hands it (the Mere) remained in a neglected state for many years; for, as before, from inattention to the cleansing of the sluice, and from the narrow passage of the flood-gates, which

were still liable to be choaked with mud, etc., and much of the out-fall being lost, the lands upon the Meer became again of little value, being covered with water all the winter, and liable to be flooded by very trivial summer rains. In this condition the best Meer lands let for a few shillings the large acre only.

"In the year 1778 I settled here; and as the most extensive and valuable wear of the Meer belonged to this estate, I had the levels taken from low-water mark; and finding a considerable fall, I had recourse to Mr. Gilbert of Worsley (who had judiciously planned and happily executed the astonishing works of his Grace the Duke of Bridgewater). To his friendship and abilities I am indebted for the success of the drainage; for, after the most minute inspection, he gave me every encouragement, and kindly assisted me in directing the undertaking. By his advice I applied to the other four proprietors of Martin Meer for a lease for the term of three lives for their several shares, and opened to them my intention of effectually draining the whole at my own expense. In 1781 I obtained the leases from the proprietors (one only excepted) and immediately began the work.

"The plan Mr. Gilbert struck out, which I have executed, was to have in the main sluice three different pairs of flood-gates. The first was to keep the sea out, which are called the Sea-gates. The second pair are erected at about half a mile distance nearer to the Meer, to stop the sea there, in case any accident should happen to the first: these are termed the stop-gates. The third pair are built close to, and in the same walls with the Sea-gates, but open and shut in a contrary direction to them: these are named the flushing-gates. All these three flood-gates are kept open, to give a

D D 2

free passage to the waters from the Meer, when the tide is sufficiently retired; and when the tide rises again above the level of the waters of the Meer, the sea-gates are shut. In dry seasons when a sufficient quantity of water does not come down from the Meer to keep the out-fall sluice open across the loose flying sands on the shore, the tide itself is permitted to flow up the sluice to the stop-gates, which are then shut; and at high water the flushing-gates are closed to keep the sea-water in.

" N.B. All these three several gates have four paddles at the bottom, three feet in length, and two feet in depth, which are drawn up by screws to flush away any obstacle that may chance to impede their working. At low water the paddles of the flushing-gates are drawn up, and the retained sea-water rushes out with so much violence that the sluice to low water is in a very short time cleansed from every obstruction, sand, mud, etc. that may have been brought up by the tide.

"Thus by the great skill and superior ingenuity of one man (Mr. Gilbert) the great obstacle to the perfect drainage of Martin Meer is done away which had baffled the many vain attempts of the proprietors for almost a century.

" By an accurate examination of the out-fall, Mr. Gilbert found it would admit the sill or threshold of the new gates being laid five inches lower than it formerly had been ; and he recommended the sea-gates to be advanced about two hundred yards nearer to the out-fall upon the open marsh. To prevent the sea flowing into the sluice behind these gates, large and strong banks are thrown up on each side, which are continued to the stop-gates ; and at the same time they answer another essential purpose, viz. by containing a larger quantity of sea-water to flush with.

" The new sea-gates are eighteen feet wide, and nineteen feet and a half high and the sill five feet lower than the former : this makes the passage in rainy seasons, when the water would have run four feet upon the sill, to bear the proportion of one hundred and sixty-two feet in the present gates, to fifty-six in the old ones.

" When we had sunk to the proper depth of the foundations of the new gates, we found a quicksand and built upon it. The walls are twelve bricks in thickness at the bottom, and there is no settlement, nor have they sunk in the least.—N.B. Large flat stones were laid under the brick and stone work and were the only preventive used.

" Whilst the gates were building, I employed all the hands I could procure in deepening and widening the sluice upon a dead level with the sill up to the Meer, six yards wide at the bottom, allowing a foot and a half slope to every foot in elevation. In some places the cutting was near twenty feet deep ; and at the depth of sixteen feet in the sand, I found an entire trunk of a tree, which squared a foot. In April 1783 the level was carried up completely to the Meer, which then (owing to the waters having been dammed up) was flooded higher than it had been for several years. As soon as the dam-head was cut, the superior efficacy of the new works appeared, and this uncommon flood ran off in five days, which would have required as many weeks to have discharged through the old floodgates. After the waters had run off, the sluice was deepened nearly to the sea-level through the lowest parts of the Meer. The sluice is nearly five miles in length from the sea-gates.

" The ditches were next attended to ; and, since the drainage, above a hundred miles in length have been perfected ; but as small open drains were necessary to carry the rain-water off into the ditches, I procured a draining or guttering plough on Mr. Cuthbert Clark's construction, which was drawn by eight, sometimes ten able horses, and which I can with certainty recommend as a most useful implement in all fenny countries. I am greatly indebted to the inventor, for with this, in one day, I cut drains nearly eight miles in length, thirteen inches in depth, twenty inches wide at the top and five at the bottom, more perfect than could have been done in that land by the hand, and which would have cost, if done by hand, seven pounds five shillings and tenpence.

" The summer of 1783 was employed wholly as above, in laying the land dry. In the year 1784 some few acres were ploughed and yielded a tolerable crop of spring corn ; some yielded a very inferior kind of hay ; the rest was pastured. . . . The effects of drainage appear from the crops ; for I have sold barley for eleven pounds, seventeen shillings and sixpence the large acres, the produce of the land which before let at no more than four shillings the acre ; and oats at ten pounds seventeen shillings and sixpence per acre, off lands, which could bring no price before ; the purchaser to cut, carry' off etc. all at his own expense.

" From the lands which before afforded a very poor pasture in the driest summers, I last year fed several head of Scotch cattle, which did better than any that were fattened upon the best grazing grounds in our neighbourhood. The best meadow lands in the most favourable seasons did not let for more than about nine shillings an acre. Last year I mowed many acres, worth three pounds, and let off several of inferior grass, at two pounds an acre, reserving the after grass for my own cattle."

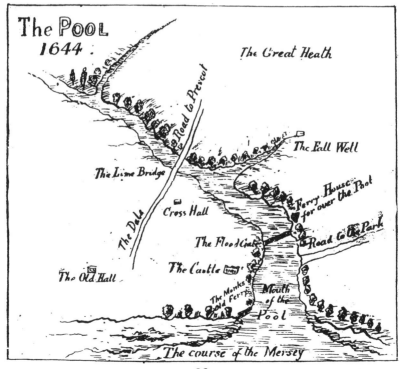

THE BEGINNINGS OF SOUTHPORT

SOUTHPORT was originally known as South Hawes, and until 1792 was "a dreary sandbank at the lower end of a bay seventeen fathoms deep, which is now choked up with sand." A certain Mr. Sutton of North Meols, who was locally nicknamed "The Duke," believed in the advantages of the spot for sea-bathing, then becoming generally fashionable owing to King-George III.'s annual visits to Weymouth. He backed his belief with his pocket, and built the Royal Hotel. This was in 1792.

Sutton's speculation was immediately dubbed "The Duke's Folly," disaster of the worst being freely predicted. But "The Duke" evidently was a far-seeing person. For six years the hotel stood in solitude, and his critics rejoiced in the fulfilment of their prophecies. At the end of that time, however, a few cottages made their appearance near the hotel, and from that year (1798) Southport has steadily progressed until to-day, when she holds the proud position of being the leading watering-place in Lancashire.

In eleven years the few cottages had grown into 38 houses with 100 inhabitants; twenty-four years afterwards the 38 houses had increased to 340, and the 100 inhabitants to 800. The next twenty-six years saw a phenomenal increase, the census returns giving the number of inhabitants as over ten thousand.

THE LIVERPOOL TRAGEDY

Or, A Warning to disobedient Children and Covetous Parents; showing how one, John Fuller, left his father's house to go to sea against his will, and was shipwrecked, but was preserved on a rock; how he was fetched by the ship's boat, and put ashore at Bengal, where he married; how he returned home, when he, not informing his parents who he was, they murdered him for the sake of his gold; with their tragical end.

PART I

YOU tender parents that have children dear,
    Be pleased to wait awhile and you shall hear
A dismal accident befel of late,
Which ought to bear an everlasting date.

At famous Liverpool, in Lancashire,
One Mr. Robert Fuller liv'd, we hear;
A grazier, who liv'd in a happy state,
He being not too poor, nor yet too great.

He had three daughters, charming beauties bright,
And but one son, which was his heart's delight;
His father doated on him, and in truth
He was a dutiful and sober youth.

He bound him 'prentice to one, Mr. Brown,
A noted surgeon who liv'd in the town;
With whom he stay'd the term of seven years,
And serv'd him faithfully, as it appears.

And afterwards some time did with him dwell,
And as a servant pleas'd his master well;
He got acquainted with a surgeon's mate,
Who was going a voyage up the Strait.

He did persuade him for to go to sea,
And said in time he might promoted be;
This so much wrought upon the young man's mind,
That he to go with him seem'd much inclined.

He went and told his father his design,
That he would go to sea in a little time,—
"For I to the East Indies now will go;
Therefore, dear father, do not say me No."

To hear these words his father was surpris'd,
It soon fetch'd tears from his aged eyes;
"Can you, my son," said he, "from me depart,
And leave me here behind with aching heart?

"Because I plac'd in you my chief delight,
Do you my tender care this way requite?
You my consent to go shall never have;
Twill bring me down with sorrow to the grave.

'Go wilful youth! Perhaps the time may come
That you may wish you'd stay'd with me at home."
But all these arguments would not prevail;
He was resolv'd the raging main to sail.

His mother cried, "I thought I had a son
Would be my comfort for the time to come."
His sisters cried, "Dear brother, do not go,
And leave our father thus oppress'd with woe."

His father said, "My son, let reason rule;
Take my advice, and do not play the fool.
What is the meaning of this sudden change?
What makes you fancy at this time to range?"

"Father! all these persuasions are in vain;
I am resolv'd to cross the raging main;
Therefore, give me your blessing ere I go,
For I'll be gone, whether you will or no."

His father cry'd, "Since you don't me regard,
God justly will your wickedness reward;
God's heavy judgment will upon you come,
For being such a disobedient son.

"So you must go without what you now crave;
Mine nor God's blessing will you ever have."

88

What course now this stubborn youth doth
    steer,
You in the second part shall quickly hear.

PART II

He went with speed unto the surgeon's
    mate
And goes with him a voyage up the Strait ;
But with that voyage he was not content ;
Further to go his rambling mind was bent.

He came to London and a ship he found,
Which lay at Deptford, for the Indies
    bound ;
And straight he ordered his matters so
As surgeon's mate on board of her to go.

The very next day, as he set sail, we hear,
He sent a letter to his father dear ;
" Father," he wrote, " I am alive 'nd well,
But when I shall return I cannot tell.

" I am on board a noble ship of fame,
For the Indies bound, the *Prince* by name ;
I will come home when my wild frolic's
    run ;
So this is all at present from your son."

His aged father read the letter strait,
And said, " My son is gone in spite of fate ;
All I can do, I'll act a father's part,
And beg of God to turn his stubborn heart."

Where now his aged father we will leave,
And turn unto his son, which made him
    grieve,
Who then was sailing on the ocean wide ;
But mark what in short time did him betide.

As by the coast of Brazil they did sail,
Boreas began to blow a blustering gale ;
The captain then, with deep concern, did
    say,
" If this storm holds, we shall be cast away."

He scarce had spoke these words, when on
    a rock,
The ship was drove with such a mighty
    shock ;
She stuck so fast she could not get away ;
So they in sorrow were there forced to stay.

The captain cried, " Let's beg of God that
    He
May from this shocking danger set us free :
Next let all hands help to heave out the
    boat,
That o'er the rolling billows we may float."

He gave command ; the thing as soon were
    done,
And overboard with speed the boat was
    flung ;
Each one to save his life got in with speed,
Until the boat would hold no more indeed.

The boat it were so full it could not swim,
So some were forcèd to get out again ;
The surgeon's mate, the grazier's stubborn
    son,
As fortune orderèd, chanced to be one.

He was obliged out of the boat to go
Back to the ship, his heart oppress'd with
    woe ;
Fifteen poor souls behind them they did
    leave,
Whose piercing cries a stony heart would
    grieve.

The captain cried, " My boat will hold no
    more ;
But if I should live to get on shore,
And you remain alive in this sad case,
I'll surely come and fetch you from this
    place."

PART III

The poor distressèd men in great despair,
Unto the Lord did make their humble
    prayer,
Expecting every minute for to be
Sunk to the bottom of the swelling sea.

The grazier's son said, " Here I will not
    stay,
But through the foamy billows swim away.
I can swim well ; the sea does calm appear ;
So fare you well my brother sailors dear."

He overboard did jump before them all,
Which made the seamen after him to call :
" You silly man, you cannot get on shore,
We think that we shall never see you more."

Thus he went along till almost night,
When his poor limbs were tired quite ;
But fortune unto him did prove so kind,
That he by chance a mighty rock did find.

The rock was rugged, high, and very steep ;
He with much trouble up the side did
    creep,
And looking round, no land he could
    behold ;
He cry'd, " My sorrow now is manifold."

"My father's words into my mind does
    come,
That I do wish I stopt with him at home ;
Also I find it true what he then said ;
But now my disobedience is repaid.

" He likewise told me if I e'er did slight
His careful counsel, God would me requite ;
He told me, though a blessing I did crave,`
His nor God's blessing I should never have."

Part IV

He thus lamenting, spent the tedious night
Until the morning it grew light ;
Then went to search the rock all round,
Where for his food some shell-fish he found.

Satan, the first deceiver of mankind,
Did come to tempt this surgeon, as we find,
Thinking he would with any terms comply,
So took advantage of his misery.

While this young surgeon looked out to sea
At a good distance from him seem'd to be
A something rowing to him in a boat,
Which o'er the rolling waves did swiftly
    float.

This young man thought he'd been a friend
    at first
But next he fear'd that it was something
    worse ;
" For if some wild man-eater it should be,
He first will kill, then next devour me."

The young man were soon freed from fear,
As the devil, like some sailor did appear ;
And when he came unto the rock did say,
" Young man, how came you here this very
    day ? "

The surgeon all his whole misfortunes told,
And while the truth to him he did unfold,
Three drops of blood down from his nose
    did fall,
Which made him think him not a friend
    withal.

The devil then reply'd, " Young man, if you
Will be my servant, wholly, just and true,
And will resign yourself all up to me,
I from this wretched place will set you
    free."

The young man found who were with him
    then,
And cried, " You grand deceiver of us men,

O get you gone, your flattery forbear
Why do you try my soul for to ensnare ?

" I now your whole temptations do despise,
Thou subtle fiend, thou father of all lies ;
I will resign myself to God alone ;
Therefore thou vile deceiver, quick, be-
    gone ! "

The devil then he strait did disappear,
And left the surgeon trembling with fear ;
Where now awhile we'll leave him to com-
    plain,
And turn unto his shipmates once again.

The captain in the boat got safe on shore,
And soon returnèd to the ship once more,
Where, out of fifteen, nine were left alive ;
The captain did their drooping hearts re-
    vive.

" Where is the rest of you ? " the captain
    cry'd
" Alas ! with hunger they have dy'd.
All but the surgeon, who here wouldn't
    stay,
And overboard did jump, and swam away."

The captain cry'd, " I hope my dream is
    right,
That he were on a rock I dreamt last night ;
So man the boat, for I the rock do know,
To save his life I thither now will go."

The boat was mann'd, and to the rock they
    came,
Where to their joy, he did alive remain ;
They took him in, and then they row'd
    away,
Which proved unto him a happy day.

Part V

Their ship from off the rock they soon did
    get,
And took great pains in well repairing it ;
Then for Bengal in India they did sail,
And soon arrivèd with a prosperous gale

The surgeon soon got him there a wife,
And ten years liv'd a very happy life ;
Six children had, likewise a good estate,
But he was born to be unfortunate.

About his parents he was troubled so,
That back to England he would go ;

90

He left his wife and children, as 'tis told,
And with him took ten hundred pounds in
gold.

Two of his sisters in that time were dead,
The other to a glazier marrièd ;
He call'd there first, she was o'erjoyed to
see
That her own brother yet alive should be.

" How does my parents do ? " then he did
say,
She cry'd, " They're well, I saw them yesterday ;
But they're so covetous grown of late,
They scarce allow themselves food for to
eat."

" This night I'll go and lodge there," he
did say ;
" But they shan't know me till you come
next day."
Unto his father's house he then did go,
Asking if he a lodging could have or no ?

They answer'd, " Yes," and bid him strait
come in,
But now, alas ! his sorrows did begin ;
His father said, " Young man, I tell you
true,
I had a son who was very much like you."

A purse of gold he to his mother gave,
And said, " To-morrow it of you I'll have."
She cry'd, " You shall." He then went to
bed,
When the devil quickly put it in her head,

To murder her own son, the gold to have,
For that was all she in this world did crave.
" Husband," said she, " When he is dead
and gone,
Then all the gold will surely be our own."

To murder this young man they both did
go,
But that he was their son they did not
know ;
They found him fast asleep, void of all care,
Then quickly cut his throat from ear to ear.

His sister came, saying, " Father dear,
Did there not come my brother here ? "
He answer'd, " No." She said, " There did
indeed."
" Alas ! " said they, " we've made our son
to bleed."

He strait took up then the bloody knife,
And instant put a period to his life :
His wife she sat a little while below,
At last upstairs did to her husband go.

Where, to her grief, she saw him bleeding
lie ;
She cry'd, " Alas ! I've causèd you to die,
All by my means, for the sake of cursed
gold :
My child and husband dead I do behold !

" Now I will make up the number three.
I cannot live such a sad sight to see."
Saying, " World, farewell ! gold, from you
I must part ; "
Then run the knife into her cruel heart.

The daughter, wond'ring at their long delay,
Did go upstairs to see what made them
stay ;
When the dreadful sight she did behold,
Her dying mother all the story told.

Then did her daughter weep, then went
away,
And raving mad, died on the next day.
So children all, from disobedience flee,
And parents, likewise, not too covetous be !

The Liverpool and Manchester Grand Railway.

THERE is an intense conservatism inherent in the English character which makes all changes a matter of bitter opposition. In our own day and generation we have witnessed the determined fight made against the introduction of motor-cars, and have heard the ribald shouts with which their first appearance in the streets, preceded by a man carrying a red flag, was greeted. Our forefathers opposed the introduction of railways with even greater bitterness, but like ourselves speedily grew accustomed to the new method of travel, and as speedily came to regard it as one of the public necessities of existence.

The precise origin of railroads is unknown, but there is little doubt that they were used by the Egyptians, the Greeks, Romans, and Assyrians for transporting the huge masses of stone used in the building of their colossal temples and palaces. In England the first mention we hear of such a railroad—or to speak more accurately, tramway, since the word "railroad" in modern parlance suggests the use of steam—is between 1602 and 1649 when some unknown and ingenious person, noticing that the ruts in a road made the work of the horses easier, applied the principle to the reduction of labour. By placing logs of wood in two parallel lines, exactly the width of the wheels of his carts apart, he made a rough tramway, by the use of which a single horse could draw forty-two hundredweight without extra fatigue in place of seventeen hundredweight. By the year 1676, these tramways from mine-heads to places of deposit were in general use in Northumberland, for Roger North, in describing a visit of his brother, Lord Guilford, the famous judge, at the close of one of his circuit visits to Newcastle, says : " When men have pieces of ground between the colliery and the river, they sell leave to lead coals over their ground, and so dear, that the owner of a rood of ground will expect twenty pounds per annum for this leave." These were called " way-leaves." Describing the method of carriage, Roger North continues: " The manner of the carriage is by laying rails of timber from the colliery down to the river, exactly straight and parallel, and bulky carts are made with four rowlets fitting these rails, whereby the carriage is so easy, that one horse will draw down four or five chaldron of coals, and is an immense benefit to the coal merchants."

Until 1738 no change was made in these wooden tramways, except perhaps in the quality of the wood. In that year, in the *Transactions of the Highland Society*, we find that " cast-iron rails were first substituted for wooden ones, but owing to the old wagons continuing to be employed, which were of too much weight for the cast iron, they did not completely succeed in the first attempt. However, about 1768, a simple contrivance was attempted, which was to make a number of smaller wagons and link them together, and, " by thus diffusing the weight of one large wagon into many, the principal cause of the failure in the first instance was removed, because the weight was more divided upon the iron." Here we have the earliest indication of the system of modern railway trucks and carriages. Three years previously there is a similar indication of our modern railroad—lines laid upon sleepers — " when the road [from the mine] has been traced at six feet in breadth, and where the declivities are fixed, an excavation is made of the breadth of the same road, more or less deep as the levelling of the road requires. There are afterwards arranged along the whole breadth of this excavation, pieces of oak wood of the thickness of four, five, six, and even eight inches square : these are placed across and at the distance of two or three feet from each other; these pieces need only be squared at their extremities, and upon these are fixed other pieces of wood well squared and sawed, of about six or seven inches' breadth by five in depth, with pegs of wood ; these pieces [the lines] are placed on each side of the road along its whole length; they are commonly placed at four feet distant from each other, which forms the interior breadth of the road."

Although the discovery of steam brought about a revolution in the cotton trade, and in every manufacturing trade in the country, its use as a locomotive force was absolutely disbelieved in. Yet, as early as 1804, there was a locomotive on a Welsh railway, drawing as many carriages as would contain ten tons of bar iron, at the rate of five miles an hour! Nevertheless for years afterwards it was gravely contended by scientific men, and even by engineers, that a locomotive could not draw heavy loads, and that the adhesion of the smooth wheels of the carriage to the smooth iron of the rails would be so slight that the wheels would simply move round in one place and have no forward movement. In spite of all demonstrations to the contrary, and George Stephenson's invention of his locomotive, this theory remained unshaken for many years.

It is one of the axioms of our civilization that there is no progress without change, and as Lancashire owed its first great leap towards prosperity to the Duke of Bridgewater and his canal, which revolutionized the carrying in the coal and iron trades, so it owed its still greater prosperity to Thomas Gray and Walter James, who first projected the Liverpool and Manchester Railway. Thomas Gray lived at Nottingham, and was " noted for what was considered a whimsical crotchet," namely, that a general system of iron railways might and ought to be laid down, on which trains of carriages drawn by locomotive steam-engines should run, and thus supersede the use of coaches, and also in a great measure canal-boats and stage-wagons for goods. This scheme, it was said, " had for years completely taken possession of and absorbed Mr. Gray's whole mind ; that it was the one great and incessant subject of his thoughts and conversation ; that begin when you would, on whatever subject—the weather, the news, the political movements of the day—it would not be many minutes before with Thomas Gray, you would be enveloped with steam, listening to an harangue on a general iron railway." Of course Thomas Gray was looked on as little better than a madman, a crotchety fellow, a dreamer, a builder of castles in the air, one of the race of discoverers of the elixir of life, the philosopher's stone, and perpetual motion. With one consent he was voted an intolerable bore. "Thomas Gray and myself came in contact," says Mr. Howarth, "and true enough he soon broke out on this railway steam along a tramroad, connecting a colliery with a wharf at which the coals were shipped, asked an engineer—

"Why are not these tramroads laid down all over England, so as to supersede our common roads, and steam-engines employed to convey goods and passengers along them, to supersede horse-power?"

"Propose that to the nation," was the

THE CUTTING AT OLIVE MOUNT SHOWING ONE OF THE FIRST TRAINS

topic: visions of railways running all over the kingdom, conveying thousands of people, and hundreds of tons of goods at a good round trot; coaches and coachmen annihilated; canals covered with duckweed; enormous fortunes made by good speculations, being talked of as sober realities that were to be."

Gray was once travelling upon business in the north of England, and seeing a small train of coal-wagons impelled by engineer's reply, "and see what you will get by it! Why, sir, you will be worried to death for your pains."

These words were actually a prophecy. Gray sent petitions to Ministers of State, he memorialized the Prime Minister, and finally petitioned the Lord Mayor and Corporation of the City of London; but it was all in vain, his scheme was flouted and disdained, and he himself regarded as little better than a madman.

But during these four years (1820–24) circumstances were gradually shaping themselves in Liverpool and Manchester, which caused the leading merchants of those two cities to lend a willing ear to Gray's proposals when he approached them. These circumstances were chiefly the unparalleled rise of the two places, and their dependence upon one another for continued prosperity, since Liverpool found a purchaser in Manchester for the raw material which was imported into its warehouses from abroad, whilst Manchester depended upon Liverpool for the supplies which kept its mills and its workpeople in full employment. The inventions of Arkwright, Hargreaves and Crompton had so increased the cotton manufacture that, in nine years only, the increase of cotton sent from Liverpool had been fifty millions of pounds. In 1790 there was one steam-engine in Manchester; in 1824 there were two hundred. The rapid increase of Liverpool and Manchester reads like a romance. In thirty-six years Liverpool had added 108,000 inhabitants to her population, whilst " the mills of Manchester contained a working population equal to many continental cities." Great fortunes were made in those days, and the following is no extravagant picture, although somewhat grandiloquent : " The capitalists of Manchester founded families, built churches, sent law-givers to the Senate, mingled their blood with that of the aristocracy, and bequeathed princely fortunes to their sons. They outdid the patricians in the purchase of estates ; and often employed more plebeians in one factory than the equestrian order could boast in its entirety. The painter found in them his most munificent patrons. The produce of the sculptor's skill graced their homes and proved their taste. They were capable of appreciating, and

were willing to support the highest aspirations of science. They were intelligent representatives of an interest which had spread with the growth of machinery throughout England. At first a clique, gathered in particular localities for a particular purpose, despised by the great landed aristocracy as the founders of their own fortunes, they expanded to a class alike antagonistic and dangerous to that power which ever refused to recognize them. The cotton lord of Manchester was then as much a feature in the history of commerce as he is now a feature in the history of the Senate. There were more opulent fortunes in the dark streets of that unrepresented town than in the fairest continental cities. There were men, too, with minds as enlarged as their fortunes, capable of grasping any subject, of advancing any capital, of embracing any practical plan."

Precisely the same words might have been written about Liverpool ; yet despite this increase of wealth and importance the carriage of goods—upon which that wealth and importance depended—was still in the hands of three canal companies : the Irwell and Mersey Navigation, the Bridgewater, and the Leeds and Liverpool Canals. During twenty-nine years (1795–1824) they had trebled their rates, and, because of their monopoly, had grown to exercise an unbearable tyranny. In these days of competition it is almost incredible to read of the agents of the canal companies holding levées attended by crowds of merchants who were admitted one by one, to implore and beg as a favour the forwarding of their goods. One firm was limited by the agents to sending sixty or seventy bags a day, and it is on record that of five thousand feet of pine timber ordered by a firm in Manchester, two thousand feet remained unshipped from November 1824 until March 1825. It frequently took a longer time for goods to come from Liverpool to Manchester than from Liverpool to New York; and although they were conveyed across the Atlantic in twenty-one days they were often kept for six weeks in the docks and warehouses at Liverpool before being taken on by the canal to Manchester.

One of the canal companies declined to carry any timber at all, another would take only one particular kind, and a third refused to carry wheat, whilst all three refused one particular kind of cotton, because of its great bulk. The canal companies exercised all the power of petty tyrants, utterly regardless of the fact that owing to their dilatoriness and limitation of quantities to be carried, thousands of workpeople were constantly deprived of a day's wages in the mills owing to the lack of supplies. The streets of Manchester were often impassable with the carts carrying timber; the warehouses and quays at Liverpool filled to overflowing.

Liverpool and Manchester seethed with indignation, and Mr. Huskisson, the statesman, put the matter very clearly before the House of Commons. "Cotton was detained a fortnight at Liverpool," he said, "while the Manchester manufacturers were obliged to suspend their labours, and goods manufactured at Manchester for foreign markets could not be transmitted in time, on account of the tardy conveyance." In vain were urgent representations made to the canal companies, in vain was it pointed out to them that they were strangling the steadily growing industries and prosperity of both places; remonstrances and representations from the leading men both of Liverpool and Manchester met only with rudeness. If the Duke of Bridgewater had been alive these merchants and manufacturers would have received a very different answer, except that there would have been no necessity for such representations, for under his management the delays and inattention would never have occurred. But the Duke himself seemed to have a prophetic instinct that railways would supersede his beloved canals: "They will last my time," he said, "but I see mischief in the d—d tramways!"

It was at this juncture that Thomas Gray approached the principal inhabitants of Liverpool and Manchester and placed before them his idea for a railway between the two great centres of shipping and manufacture, his views being set forth in a book entitled: "Observations on a general iron railway, or land steam-conveyance, to supersede the necessity for horses in all public vehicles; shewing its vast superiority in every respect over the present pitiful methods of conveyance by turnpike roads, canal and coasting tenders. Containing every species of information relative to railroads and locomotive engines. By Thomas Gray.

"'No speed with this can fleetest horse compare,
No weight like this canal or vessel bear:
As this will commerce every way promote,
To this let sons of commerce grant their vote.'"

Amongst the many benefits set forth in this book was that the mails from London to Liverpool and Manchester might be conveyed within the space of twelve hours.

Thomas Gray, however, had a rival in his suggestion of the Liverpool and Manchester Railway, William James of Snowford Manor, a rival to whom many declared the honour of the project was due. James made a survey between Liverpool and Manchester in 1822, but his plan was abandoned. He was a most ardent supporter of a railway system, and pursued the cause "with a missionary zeal, though not with a missionary's salary." As a matter of fact he beggared himself in his efforts to bring his plans to completion. The honour actually lies equally between these two men—William James projected *a* Liverpool and Manchester Railway, Thomas Gray directly brought about *the* Liverpool and Manchester Railway.

Mr. Sandars, of Liverpool, paid ten pounds a mile (£300) for James's survey; but, as has been said, the scheme was abandoned—this was partly on account of the engineering difficulties, and because the opposition of the landowners, through whose property the line would pass, had been roused by the canal proprietors, who in their insolence of monopoly suddenly found themselves face to face with an unrealized danger. But, so far as the canal was concerned, the writing was on the wall. "The annoyance to which the commerce of Liverpool had been subjected, the difficulties which the manufacturers (of Manchester) had encountered, the pecuniary loss, the mental irritation, together, probably, with a great increase of unemployed capital combined to bring about that extraordinary change in locomotion." A declaration that a new line of communication was necessary between the two places was signed by one hundred and fifty merchants, and a meeting was held at Liverpool at which a railway—the first of its kind in England—was determined upon. But before proceeding any further a formal application was made to the canal agents to reduce the charges and increase the accommodation. A definite and unqualified refusal was given. The agents were then told that if no extra assistance were given by the canals, the capitalists of Liverpool and Manchester would build a railway between the two towns.

Railways had been so much talked about that they had developed into a sort of "if pigs had wings they could fly." They were regarded as the dreams of madmen, and when the canal agents were offered shares in the new undertaking, they contemptuously answered, "All or none." "So blind were those responsible for the management of the canals to the forces that were slowly but steadily rising against them, that they scouted the very notion of the smallest reduction; they wallowed in their dividends with a confidence that must always be impolitic and presumptuous when not perfectly secure; they engendered the elements of that opposition they at first ridiculed but now respect; and they frittered away their concession in a manner that excited the mirth of their opponents and the pity of their friends."

The first prospectus of the Liverpool and Manchester Railway was issued on October 29, 1824, and attached to it were the names of the leading merchants and shippers of Manchester and Liverpool. It presented an overwhelming case against the canals: "It is competition that is wanted, and the proof of this assertion," says the prospectus, "may be deduced from the fact that the shares in the old Quay Navigation, of which the original cost was seventy pounds, have been sold as high as one thousand two hundred and fifty pounds." It goes on to state: "The canal establishments are inadequate for the great object to be attempted—the regular and punctual conveyance of goods at all seasons and periods. In the summertime there is frequently a deficiency of water, obliging boats to go only half loaded. In winter they are sometimes loaded up for weeks together." The opposition of the landowners was met with the explanation: "The road does not approach within about a mile of the residence of the Earl of Sefton, and traverses the Earl of Derby's property over barren mosses, passing about two miles from the Hall." It was stated in the prospectus that the total quantity of merchandise passing between Liverpool and Manchester was one thousand two hundred tons a day, the average time of passage being thirty-six hours, and the average charge fifteen shillings a ton! A comparison between these figures and those of to-day puts the stupendous growth of the trade between the two cities in a nutshell.

which could affect the scheme adversely were spread against it. Landowners were told that the smoke would kill their birds as they flew over the loco-motive. The manufacturer was told that the sparks from its chimney would burn his mills. Foxes and pheasants would cease in the neighbourhood of a railway. Farmers were told that the race of horses would be extinguished, and that oats and hay would no longer be market-able produce, whilst it was even said that cows would cease to yield their milk in

SECOND AND THIRD CLASS CARRIAGES

The prospectus created the greatest interest throughout the whole of England, and an application was made to the House of Commons to grant a Bill. But, despite the fact that Mr. Huskisson's word was beyond reproach, the Bill met with the most determined opposition. He stated " that the promoters of the scheme had a higher object than the mere accumulation of wealth through this channel. They would render a great commercial benefit to this country. The subscribers were the mer-chants, bankers, traders and manufacturers of Liverpool and Manchester. They had agreed that no person should hold more than ten shares each. He had seen the parties interested, and they had declared they were willing to limit the amount of dividends to ten per cent., and that they would be perfectly satisfied with five per cent." Every report and every rumour

the neighbourhood of one of these infernal machines.

The general feeling of the public towards railways can be gauged by this pronounce-ment in *The Quarterly*, the most serious of all the reviews : " The greatest exag-geration of the powers of the locomotive steam-engine, or, to speak more plainly, the steam-carriage, may delude for a time, but must end in the mortification of those concerned. It is certainly some consola-tion to those who are to be whirled at the rate of eighteen or twenty miles an hour, by means of the high-pressure engine, to be told that they are in no danger of being sea-sick while they are on shore, that they are not to be scalded to death, nor burned by the bursting of the boiler, and that they need not mind being shot by the scattered fragments, or dashed in pieces by the flying off or breaking of a wheel."

When the Bill went into Committee it was made the subject of a general attack, the greatest severity of which was directed against George Stephenson; and the Exchange of Liverpool was denounced for having aided and abetted the prospector's plan. "It was the most absurd scheme that ever entered the head of man to conceive"; said one. Another "would sooner give ten thousand pounds than have the steam-engine come puffing near him," and it was called "the greatest strain upon human credulity ever heard of." Market-gardeners would be ruined; the value of land would be lowered, and steam would vanish before frost and storm.

The Bill failed to pass the Commons after a discussion of thirty-seven days, chiefly because of certain errors in the survey made by George Stephenson. The errors were brought about by the opposition of the landowners, which had caused him to take the survey secretly; and he was accused of having "trodden down the corn of widows, destroyed the strawberry beds of gardeners, committed trespasses and violated private rights."

The promoters of the railway, in no way daunted by this failure of their plans, immediately set about making a new survey and a new prospectus. In this prospectus special care was taken to lessen the opposition of the great landowners, particularly of Lord Sefton, who had strongly opposed the Bill. The new route entirely avoided his estate; whilst it touched only a few detached fields of the estate of another opponent, Lord Derby. "Far removed from the Knowsley domain, the Committee have to state," said the prospectus, "that they have spared no pains to accommodate the exact route to the wishes of proprietors whose estates they cross, by removing the route to a distance from the mansions of proprietors, and

from those portions of estates more particularly appropriated to game preserves." But the most important part of the prospectus was the announcement that the Marquis of Stafford had taken one thousand shares in the company for himself, and those of his family who were beneficially interested in the Duke of Bridgewater's Canal. This public support of the Marquis of Stafford was of the greatest help to the promoters of the railway, but still the storm of opposition was not entirely silenced. The streets through which the line was to pass rose against it; the old Quay Company objected to a bridge being built over the Irwell, whilst the Leeds and Liverpool Canal objected to the railway passing in a tunnel beneath their stream. With the greatest tact and discretion the streets which objected were avoided; and the objection of the companies was met by the line neither crossing the canal nor tunnelling under the river.

Once more the Bill for a railway between Liverpool and Manchester was introduced to Parliament, and once more the most absurd arguments were brought against it. One Member of Parliament undertook to prove that the journey would take ten hours, and that the train could only be worked by horses. Another said "he would not consent to see widows' premises invaded, and how would any person like to have a railway line under his parlour window." It is difficult in these days to imagine the House of Commons being solemnly asked "if it was aware of the smoke and the noise, the hiss and the whirl, which locomotive engines passing on the road at ten or twelve miles an hour would occasion," and being informed that "a railroad would be the greatest nuisance, the most complete disturbance of the quiet and comfort of the kingdom that the ingenuity of man

99

could invent." Notwithstanding the most determined opposition, the Bill passed, and on September 15, 1830, a most memorable day in the history of English railways, the Liverpool and Manchester line was officially opened. People flocked from far and near to see the great undertaking, and amongst them was the great Duke of Wellington.

Before the great day, however, there were various trial trips upon the line ; and writing to a friend, from Liverpool on August 26, 1830, Fanny Kemble—the daughter of John Kemble, the great actor—gives a vivid description of her first experience : " A party of sixteen persons were ushered into a large courtyard, where, under cover, stood several carriages of a peculiar construction, one of which was prepared for our reception. It was a long-bodied vehicle with seats placed across it, back to back ; the one we were in held six of these benches, and was a sort of uncovered *char-à-banc*. The wheels were placed upon two iron bands which formed the road, and to which they are fitted, being so constructed as to slide along without any danger of hitching or becoming displaced, on the same principle as a thing sliding on a concave groove. The carriage was set in motion by a mere push, and having received this impetus, rolled with us down an inclined plane into a tunnel which forms the entrance to the railroad. This tunnel is four hundred yards long (I believe) and will be lighted with gas. At the end of it we emerged from darkness, and the ground becoming level, we stopped. . . . We were introduced to the little engine which was to draw us along the rails. She (for they make these curious little fire-horses all mares) consisted of a boiler, a stove, a small platform, a bench, and behind the bench enough water to prevent her being thirsty for fifteen miles — the whole

machine not bigger than a common fire-engine. She goes upon two wheels, which are her feet, and are moved by bright steel legs called pistons. These are propelled by steam, and in proportion as more steam is applied to the upper extremities (the hip-joints, I suppose) of these pistons the faster move the wheels ; and when it is desirable to diminish the speed, the steam, which unless suffered to escape would burst the boiler, evaporates through a safety-valve in the air. The reins, bit and bridle of this wonderful beast is a small steel handle, which applies or withdraws the steam from its legs or pistons, so that a child might manage it. The coals, which are its oats, are under the bench, and there is a small glass tube attached to the boiler, with water in it, which indicates by its fullness or emptiness when the creature wants water, which is immediately conveyed to it from its reservoirs. There is a chimney to the stove, but as they burn coke, there is none of the dreadful black smoke which accompanies the progress of a steam-vessel."

The sprightly writer had the honour of being taken for fifteen miles along the railroad on the engine itself by George Stephenson, who explained to her how he had got over the difficulty of carrying the railway over Chat Moss. First a foundation of hurdles—or as Stephenson called it, basket-work—was thrown over the morass, the interstices being filled with moss and heather, upon this clay and soil were laid down ; " and the road *does* float," adds Fanny Kemble, " for we passed over it at the rate of five-and-twenty miles an hour, and saw the stagnant swamp water trembling on the surface of the soil on either side of us."

Fanny Kemble was one of those who made the historical first journey from Liverpool to Manchester by train, upon which Mr. Huskisson, the Member for Liverpool, was killed.

" I will tell you something of the events of the 15th," she says in another letter, "as though you may be acquainted with the circumstances of poor Mr. Huskisson's death, none but an eye-witness of the whole scene can form a conception of it. I told you we had places given to us, and it was the main purpose of our returning from Birmingham to Manchester to be present at what promised to be one of the most striking events in the scientific annals of our country. We started on Wednesday last, to the number of eight hundred people, in carriages constructed as I have described to you. The most intense curiosity and excitement prevailed, and though the weather was uncertain, enormous masses of densely packed people lined the road, shouting and waving hats and handkerchiefs as we flew by them. What with the sight and sound of these cheering multitudes and the tremendous velocity with which we bore past them, my spirits rose to the true champagne height, and I never enjoyed anything so much as the first hour of our progress. I had been unluckily separated from my mother in the first distribution of places, but by an exchange of seats which she was enabled to make she rejoined me when I was at the height of my ecstasy, which was considerably damped by finding her frightened to death, and intent upon nothing but devising some means of escaping from a situation which appeared to her to threaten with instant annihilation, herself, and all her travelling companions. While I was chewing the cud of this disappointment—which was rather bitter, as I had expected her to be as delighted as myself with our excursion —a man flew by us, calling out through a speaking-trumpet to stop the engine, for that somebody in the directors' carriage had sustained an injury. We were all stopped accordingly, and presently a hundred voices were heard exclaiming that Mr. Huskisson was killed. The confusion that ensued is indescribable : the calling out from carriage to carriage to ascertain the truth, the contrary reports which were sent back to us, the hundred questions eagerly uttered at once, and the repeated and urgent demands for surgical assistance, created a sudden turmoil that was quite sickening. At last we distinctly ascertained that the unfortunate man's thigh was broken. · From Lady Wilton, who was in the Duke's carriage, and within three yards of the spot where the accident happened, I had the following details, the horror of witnessing which we were spared through our situation behind the great carriage" [one especially built for the Duke of Wellington and his party] : " The engine had stopped to take in a supply of water, and several of the gentlemen in the directors' carriage had jumped out to look about them. Lord Wilton,[1] Count Batthyany, Count Matuscenitz, and Mr. Huskisson, among the rest, were standing talking in the middle of the road, when an engine on the other line, which was parading up and down merely to show its speed, was seen coming down upon them like lightning. The most active of those in peril sprang back into their seats : Lord Wilton saved his life only by rushing behind the Duke's carriage, and Count Matuscenitz had but just leaped into it, with the engine all but touching his heels as he did so; while poor Mr. Huskisson, less active from the effects of age and ill-health, bewildered too by the frantic cries of ' Stop the engine ! Clear the track !' that resounded on all sides, completely lost his head, looked helplessly to the right and left, and was instantaneously

[1] He was known in society as "The Wicked Earl of Wilton."

prostrated by the fatal machine, which dashed down like a thunderbolt upon him, and passed over his leg, smashing and mangling it in the most horrible way (Lady Wilton said she distinctly heard the crushing of the bone). So terrible was the effect of the appalling the caution was repeated in the printed directions. But when the train stopped at Parkside to take in fresh water, most of the gentlemen in the carriage called the " Northumbria," in which the directors and distinguished guests had been placed, either misunderstanding or ignoring the

OPENING

OF THE

Liverpool and Manchester Railway,

15th September, 1830.

THE BARGE to convey the Company to THE WARRINGTON AND NEWTON RAILWAY STAND at Sankey Viaduct, will leave Bewsey Lock at a Quarter-past Eight o'Clock in the Morning precisely.

Subscribers not going by the Barge, are requested to be at the Stand not later than Half-past Ten, as the Procession is expected to arrive about that Time.

Holders of Tickets will be allowed to enter the Barge on shewing their Tickets, which will have to be delivered up at the Stand. No other Persons than holders of Tickets will, on any account, be permitted to go upon the Barge or the Stand.

Refreshments will be provided.

By Order,

JOHN WILSON,

CHAIRMAN.

Warrington & Newton }
Railway Office, }
13th September, 1830. }

accident that, except that ghastly ' crushing' and poor Mrs. Huskisson's piercing shriek, not a sound was heard or a word uttered among the immediate spectators of the catastrophe."

The official account of this tragedy, which so sadly marred the opening of the railway, differs in certain essentials from Fanny Kemble's. The company had been requested not to leave their carriages, and warning, got out, and stood about in groups upon the line. Suddenly an alarm was given that the " Rocket " engine was approaching, and the little groups rushed for safety, some sheltering themselves beneath the embankment, others forcing themselves into the nearest carriages. Mr. Huskisson alone hesitated, and instead of crossing the line to the embankment, or entering any other carriage, he hurried to the "Northumbria," and, taking hold of the door, tried to climb to the step. The door swung back, and the statesman fell with his legs across the line—with the terrible consequences described by Fanny Kemble.

"Lord Wilton," she continues, "was the first to raise the poor sufferer, and calling to aid his surgical skill, which is considerable, he tied up the severed artery, and for a time at least, prevented death by loss of blood. Mr. Huskisson was then placed in a carriage with his wife and Lord Wilton, and the engine having been detached from the directors' carriage, conveyed them to Manchester.[1] So great was the shock produced upon the whole party by this event, that the Duke of Wellington declared his intention not to proceed, but to return immediately to Liverpool. However, upon its being represented to him that "the whole population of Manchester had turned out to witness the procession, and that a disappointment might give rise to riots and disturbances, he consented to proceed, and gloomily enough the rest of the journey was accomplished."

In her *Records of a Girlhood* Fanny Kemble gives a description of the continuation of the journey, and the arrival at Manchester : "After this disastrous event the day became overcast, and as we neared Manchester the sky became cloudy and dark, and it began to rain. The vast concourse of people, who had assembled to witness the arrival of the successful travellers, was of the lowest order of mechanics and artisans, among whom great distress and a dangerous spirit of discontent with the Government at that time prevailed. Groans and hisses greeted the carriageful of influential personages,

---

[1] He was taken to the Vicarage at Eccles, where he died at nine o'clock that night, after suffering great agony.

in which the Duke of Wellington sat. High above the grim and grimy crowd of smiling faces a loom had been erected at which sat a tattered, starved-looking weaver, evidently set there as a *representative man*, to protest against the triumph of machinery, and the gain and the glory which the wealthy Liverpool and Manchester men were likely to derive from it. The contrast between our departure from Liverpool and our arrival at Manchester was one of the most striking things I ever witnessed. A terrible cloud covered the national achievement, and its success, which in every respect was complete, was atoned for by the Nemesis of good fortune, by the sacrifice of the first financial statesman of the country."

Although the line was only thirty miles in length, some idea of the nature of the task forced upon Stephenson and the directors may be gathered from the fact that, independently of culverts and footways, there were sixty-three bridges, thirty of which passed under the turnpike road, and twenty-eight over it ; one over the river Irwell, and four over other streams. Besides the tunnels, there was the quaking bog of Chat Moss to be crossed. When the Bill for the railway was brought before the Committee of the House of Commons this question was put to George Stephenson : "There is rock to be excavated to a depth of more than sixty feet ; there are embankments to be made nearly the same height ; there is a swamp of five miles in length to be traversed, in which if you drop an iron rod it sinks and disappears ; how will you do all this ?" In his broad Northumbrian accent, Stephenson replied, "I can't tell you *how* I'll do it, but I can tell you I *will* do it !" They dismissed him as a visionary, and the Bill as a dream of visionaries ; but nevertheless Stephenson made the railway.

One curious fact must be mentioned. Although the railway had been built primarily for the conveyance of merchandise, it was found that the revenue from passenger traffic was double that of the goods traffic. Within fourteen days of its opening the passengers amounted to 800 a day. Two years afterwards it carried 356,000 people, and in 1855 no less than 473,000. One of the immediate effects of the railway was to cheapen sugar and many other articles for the poor.

In the wondrous romance of the growth of Manchester and Liverpool, the Duke of Bridgewater created the first chapter with his canal; the intrepid merchants of the two cities created the second chapter themselves, when, in the face of the most determined opposition they brought into being the Manchester and Liverpool Railway.

A PEN-AND-INK SKETCH OF THE DUKE OF WELLINGTON

THE STRANGE CASE OF MISS M'AVOY

Dr. Renwick, who was of some eminence —went so far as to publish a pamphlet in which he not only gave evidence of her powers but expressed his entire belief in this " new and supernatural faculty."

Miss M'Avoy, encouraged by such support, rose to higher flights. She declared that by placing her fingers behind her upon the glass of a window she could see objects at a distance ; and it was gravely announced that whilst in this position, with her back to the window, she had described the figures of people in the churchyard opposite the house, as well as the colour of their clothes. This amazing assertion roused suspicion, which was further strengthened when it was found that the interposition of any substance between her face and her hands deprived her of the faculty of seeing, as it were, by touch. She explained this by saying that her breath must have free and uninterrupted communication with her hands. An ingenious gentleman, however, contrived a mask which, whilst entirely covering the face and the eyes, left the mouth free, and in no way interfered with the breathing. He offered to pay twenty guineas and another gentleman offered to pay forty guineas, if Miss M'Avoy could read a single line of moderately sized print whilst wearing the mask. There was a good deal of shilly-shallying, and finally Miss M'Avoy declined to undergo the test. Naturally, she was regarded as an impostor, which, despite Dr. Renwick's belief in her " new and supernatural faculty," she undoubtedly was. It was evident she was not entirely blind, and a mirror on the wall opposite the window had enabled her to see people in the churchyard, whilst standing with her back to the street with her fingers placed upon the glass. Her pretended reading

ALL Liverpool was in a state of excitement during the summer of 1817 over the curious case of Miss M'Avoy, a young girl of seventeen who lived in St. Paul's Square, and who, although entirely blind, was said to be able to read print and distinguish colours by touch. She had become blind in that year through an attack of hydrocephalus which was accompanied by partial paralysis.

She gave demonstrations of this faculty of touch to all and sundry, and in order to dispel any doubts as to her still having the use of her eyes, she wore a bandage over them. The house was crowded daily with people anxious to see this wonder, and the fact that no money was asked for or given, as well as the respectable position of her parents, added to the belief in her singular powers. Many wonderful accounts were published of her capacity for deciphering the smallest print, and detecting the most delicate colours in absolute darkness, as well as in the light, with her eyes bandaged. One doctor—

of small print, and the detection of colours by touch can also be accounted for by the simple fact that she actually saw them; but how she managed to perform the same feats in absolute darkness was her own secret. Since monetary gain was clearly not her object, her absurd pretensions were in all probability bred of an hysterical desire for notoriety. She certainly succeeded, for during the summer of 1817, Miss M'Avoy and her marvellous gifts were the sole topic of conversation in Liverpool. A couple of centuries earlier she would have been burnt as a witch.

ANCIENT LANDMARKS

TWO curious wooden landmarks used to stand upon the shore at Bootle-cum-Linacre to serve as a guide to mariners about to enter the Mersey. They were pulled down in the early part of the nineteenth century to make way for the new docks which were then built. These double landmarks were common all round the coast, where there was danger of approach, seafarers knowing that by steering in a line directly between the two landmarks, they were following a safe channel. The practice of marking the fairway by buoys becoming more and more prevalent the necessity for landmarks ceased to exist. Those at Bootle had shown their diamond-headed tops to approaching ships for two centuries—perhaps longer—when they were removed.

ANCIENT WOODEN LANDMARK AT BOOTLE-CUM-LINACRE

THE FIRST STANLEY EARL OF DERBY

THE story of the Stanley who became first Earl of Derby over four hundred years ago reads like a romance by an old chronicler. He was a remarkable man who made a great career, a career which had direct results upon his fellow-countrymen, but at the outset it must be admitted that he was a genius amongst time-servers. No one in the whole course of English history has sat upon the fence with such signal success as Thomas Stanley, first Earl of Derby.

The Stanley family had their origin in Staffordshire, their home being at Staneleigh—the Anglo-Saxon for stony lea—whence they took their name. Originally they were a branch of the Audley family which was founded in the reign of Henry I., and a grandson of the first Lord Audley, called William, having acquired Staneleigh by an exchange of land with his uncle, became known as William de Staneleigh. This was afterwards corrupted into Stanley. The new family owed much of its prosperity to advantageous marriages. In the time of Edward II., the son of William de Staneleigh married the daughter and co-heiress of Sir Peter Bamville, by which he became owner of a part of the manor of Storeton in Cheshire and hereditary bailiff of the forest that then covered the peninsula of Wirral, between the estuaries of the Mersey and the Dee. The bailiff of a forest was the chief ranger, and it was because of this office that the Stanleys had the right to place the three bucks' heads upon their coat of arms, which have remained unchanged.

Another William de Stanley, a descendant of the bailiff of Wirral Forest, married the heiress of Hooton, an estate about half-way between Chester and Birkenhead, and the Stanleys of Storeton became the Stanleys of Hooton. But it was this William's younger brother, John, who founded the greatness of his family. He too married an heiress, Isabel, the daughter of Sir Thomas de Lathom, and in right of his wife became the owner of Lathom and of Knowsley. Before his marriage John Stanley had made a good impression at Court; afterwards he was taken into high favour by Richard II., who made him Lord Deputy of Ireland and gave him grants of land in that country. By an unusual circumstance when Richard was deposed Sir John Stanley was taken into even higher favour by his successor Henry IV., who in place of Lord Deputy made him Lord Lieutenant of Ireland. And when the Percies —the Earl of Northumberland and his son—revolted against Henry and were routed, he gave Stanley the Lordship of the Isle of Man, with such absolute powers that the position of himself and his descendants in the island was exactly that of sovereign princes. Henry V. continued his father's favour, and appointed Sir John as Lord Lieutenant of Ireland. He died in 1413, " having during his long life raised his family from simple country gentlemen to the head of the lesser baronage." His son John was not in any way remarkable, except that he kept together all that his father had gained, but his son Thomas was distinguished both as a warrior and a diplomatist. He, like his grandfather, was Lord Lieutenant of Ireland, and a year after the breaking out of the Wars of the Roses was made a peer under the title of Baron Stanley.

Three years later he died, and was succeeded by his son Thomas, who was afterwards the first Earl of Derby, and of whom it has been justly said, " The first Stanley Earl of Derby lived in a chaotic and turbulent age, an age, too, in which the old spirit of chivalry was being superseded by modern craft and subtlety. The courage and skill of the warrior had still their value, but strength of arm and hosts of retainers were insufficient without astuteness of head, without a watchful dexterity in remaining neuter when neutrality was the safest course, or in shifting from this course to that so as to be on the winning side in times when the vanquished of yesterday might become the victor of to-day. The first Stanley Earl of Derby pursued this policy with consummate skill, reaping as a reward large additional domains and a peerage, in our own age as in his own, one of the foremost in England."

In his two marriages Thomas Stanley showed the greatest prudence and discernment from a worldly point of view.

His first wife was the daughter of Richard Neville, Earl of Salisbury, and the sister of the great Earl of Warwick, the King-maker, and the most powerful nobleman in England. At that time Warwick's great influence was all on the side of the Yorkists, and although a peace had been patched up between the two contesting parties in 1458, the war burst out in the following year with even greater violence. On his father's death in the same year Lord Stanley found himself at the head of the retainers of his house, but whilst he was quite ready to profit by the position of the relations brought by his marriage, he was too wary to commit himself to any dangerous course for the benefit of those relations. And in the very year of his succession to the title and estates he gave convincing proof of the policy he pursued throughout his life.

His father-in-law, the Earl of Salisbury, with a force of five thousand men, attacked and utterly defeated a force commanded by the Lancastrian Lord Audley (of whose family the Stanleys were originally on offshoot) for Henry VI. at Bloreheath in Staffordshire. Lord Stanley, who was only six miles away and had a force of two thousand men with him, was summoned by the King to Lord Audley's assistance. But he was too clever to commit himself to either side, and in the following year a petition was presented to Henry VI. by the Parliament impeaching and accusing Stanley of various matters set out in great detail, and praying that he might be committed to prison. The chief accusation against him was thus set forth :—

" To the King, our Sovereign Lord, show the Commons in this present Parliament assembled : That whereas it pleased your Highness to send to the Lord Stanley, by the servant of the same Lord from Nottingham, charging him that upon his faith and (al) legiance, he should come to your Highness in all haste, with such fellowship" (*i. e.* following) " as he might make, the said Lord Stanley notwithstanding came not to you, but William Stanley, his brother, went with many of the said Lord's servants and tenants, (a) great number of people, to the Earl of Salisbury which were with the same Earl at the distressing of your true liege people at Bloreheath."

Stanley had also received a summons from Henry's son, the Prince of Wales, to which he had answered that he was not ready, and in further condemnation the Parliament pointed out that he had already received the King's command to be ready at a day's notice, before he received the Prince of Wales's summons. Stanley's inaction they openly put down as the cause of the Bloreheath disaster. But the most damning fact against him was the last clause of the impeachment.

" Also whereas certain persons being of livery and clothing of the said Lord Stanley were taken at the Forest of Morff in Shropshire, the day before their death (they) confessed that they were commanded in the name and behalf of the said Lord Stanley to attend and wait upon the said William Stanley, to assist the said Earl of Salisbury in such matter (s) as he intended to execute."

It is quite clear from this document that Lord Stanley kept both sides quiet with promises of support and sympathy, whilst he carefully abstained from assisting either his king or his father-in-law, and that his brother Sir William Stanley openly joined the Earl of Salisbury. In reply to the petition of the House of Commons praying for the punishment or trial of Stanley,

Henry sent a non-committal answer in the old formula *Le roi s'avisera*—The King will consider the matter—which may have been the result of further assurances of loyalty from Lord Stanley, or have come from his fear of rendering the powerful Stanley family openly disaffected to the Lancastrian cause. Lord Stanley had not actually joined the rebels, which left a loophole both for himself and the King. The other nobles and gentlemen who had supported the Earl of Salisbury, including Sir William Stanley, were proclaimed traitors and their estates declared to be confiscated.

Lord Stanley took a solemn oath of allegiance to Henry VI. in the December of the year he had been impeached by the Commons, and a few months afterwards was employed by that monarch in an important commission, part of which was to hold in safe custody and bring to the King's presence, his two brothers-in-law John and Thomas Neville, sons of the Earl of Salisbury, and others " being in ward by the King's commandment for divers matters."

The following year, 1461, brought a change in the whirligig of events. At Towton, one of the bloodiest battles of the Wars of the Roses ended in the victory of the Yorkists, and Edward IV. mounted the throne, the Lancastrian Henry VI. being imprisoned in the Tower of London. With the Yorkist success Lord Stanley, conveniently forgetting his oath of allegiance in December 1459 to Henry VI., ceased to be Lancastrian in his sympathies : in the second year of Edward IV.'s reign he was appointed Justice of Chester.

Lord Stanley's brother-in-law, Warwick the King-maker, had placed Edward IV. on the throne. After eight years, Warwick began to plot for the restoration of poor Henry VI., whom he had himself dethroned.[1]　But Edward acted swiftly. He crushed an insurrection instigated by Warwick, and the latter hastened to Manchester to seek the aid of his brother-in-law, Lord Stanley. It was refused. The skilful time-server would not commit himself, yet when only a few months afterwards Warwick was triumphant and Edward IV. was in exile, Lord Stanley's name appears in the list of noblemen who accompanied Warwick the King-maker to the Tower of London to release Henry VI. from his imprisonment, and who followed him as he was taken " with great pomp, apparelled in a long gown of blue velvet, through the streets of London to St. Paul's."

The weak, well-meaning Henry VI.—the saddest of political victims—reigned again for some seventeen months, then the wheel of fortune turned once more. Edward IV. returned from his exile, and at the Battle of Barnet (April 14, 1471) not only were the Lancastrians defeated, but the King-maker, fighting in desperation on foot, was slain. Ten days later, the Battle of Tewkesbury put an end to the hopes and the cause of the Lancastrians. After an overwhelming defeat, Henry's son, the Prince of Wales, fell a prisoner into the hands of the Yorkists and was stabbed to death in Edward's tent. In less than a month afterwards Henry himself " died " in the Tower of London ; and Edward IV. reigned securely in his stead. But the change of king meant no change of fortune for the astute Lord Stanley, for he was soon in higher favour than before, and was made Steward of the King's Household, then a post of great confidence.

It was at this moment of his fortunes that Lord Stanley made his second marriage, the lady being Margaret Beaufort, Countess of Richmond, the mother of the

[1] See " Holy King Henry."

future King of England, Henry VII. This second marriage shows the consideration in which Lord Stanley was held, for the Countess of Richmond was the great-granddaughter of John o' Gaunt, Duke of Lancaster, her grandfather, John Earl of Somerset, having been a son of that great Prince by his mistress, Catherine Swynford, whom he afterwards married, and his children by whom were made legitimate by an Act of Parliament. Such was the power of princes in the reign of Edward III. and Richard II. !

At the age of fourteen Margaret Beaufort had married Edmund Tudor, Earl of Richmond, who was the step-brother of Henry VI., his father, the handsome Owen Tudor, having married Queen Katharine of Valois, the widow of Henry V. and the mother of Henry VI., a marriage which caused a considerable sensation, even in those easy-going times. Two months before the birth of their son, Edmund Tudor died, therefore the future Henry VII. was actually born Earl of Richmond. Some chronicles state that Margaret was not yet fourteen when she gave birth to this son. About the time when Lord Stanley was being impeached for his failure to obey Henry VI.'s summons to Bloreheath, the Countess of Richmond married Sir Henry Stafford, son of the Duke of Buckingham, who dying in 1451, left her once more a widow.

Margaret's position was one of difficulty, if not of actual danger. Her son, Henry of Richmond, had been brought up in Wales, by his uncle Jasper Tudor, Earl of Pembroke. After the murder of the Prince of Wales and the death of Henry VI., the young Earl of Richmond was the head of the house of Lancaster through his mother's descent from John o' Gaunt, consequently he was an object of suspicion and jealousy to the Yorkist Edward IV., who saw in the young man not only a possible, but a probable rival. His life, therefore, was not safe in England, and he and his uncle Jasper fled to France, where they remained—at the Court of the Duke of Brittany—throughout the whole of Edward's reign. Edward more than once made attempts to secure the young man's person, protesting to the Duke of Brittany that he meant him no harm, nor desired to keep him a prisoner, only wishing to marry him to one of his daughters. On one occasion, it is said, the Duke had actually handed the young man over to an English embassy, when he was persuaded to revoke the order and Henry was released. There is little doubt as to the fate that would have befallen Henry of Richmond if he had fallen into the ruthless hands of Edward IV. England would have had a different history, and so also would the House of Stanley.

THOMAS STANLEY, FIRST EARL OF DERBY

As the mother of a possible rival to the throne, the Countess of Richmond had a difficult part to play. Her marriage with Lord Stanley was a safeguard for herself, as she gained a powerful protector high in the favour of the Yorkist King, while as for Lord Stanley the alliance not only added immensely to his wealth and possessions, but ensured him the favour, which he afterwards held, of the Countess's son, should he ever come to the throne. On both sides it was a marriage of convenience, but the Countess is said to have

gained great influence over Lord Stanley, and to this influence in all probability may be traced the accession of the Tudor dynasty to the throne of England.

With the death of Edward IV. in 1483 came another of those sanguinary embroglios out of which, whilst others lost their lives or estates, or both, Lord Stanley soared triumphant. The Court was divided into three parties, that of the Queen-mother, Elizabeth Woodville, to which Lord Stanley belonged, and a party headed by Lord Hastings, the friend and most trusted councillor of the dead monarch, which was loyal to the boy-king Edward V., but distrustful of Richard, Duke of Gloucester, and opposed to the pretensions of the Queen-mother and her kinsfolk; and the third, the party of the Duke of Gloucester, who was already aspiring to be Protector, if not actually King.

Richard of Gloucester acted swiftly and swept away both the opposing parties. With the consent and approval of Lord Hastings, Queen Elizabeth Woodville's brother and his nephew were arrested and executed. This disposed of the first party. Hastings's turn came next without any warning. During a Council meeting in the Tower of London, at which Lord Hastings and Lord Stanley were present, Richard suddenly struck his hand upon the table, whereupon armed men rushed into the room, and, seizing Hastings, bore him away to instant execution, a plank of wood, it is said, serving as a block. On this occasion Lord Stanley, who was on terms of close friendship with the unfortunate Hastings, had the narrowest escape for his life. "In the bustle," says Sir Thomas More (that is of the armed men rushing in), "which was all before contrived, a certain person struck at the Lord Stanley with a poleaxe, and had certainly cleft him down, had he not been aware of the blow and sunk under the table. Yet he was wounded on the head that the blood ran about his ears."

This was on the 13th of June, 1483 ; on the 26th of June, Richard, Duke of Gloucester, was proclaimed King, and the very day afterwards Lord Stanley appeared as a trusted counsellor of the usurper and witnessed the monarch's formal delivery of the Great Seal of England to his Chancellor, the Bishop of London. At Richard's coronation, which took place on July 6, " the Lord Stanley bare the mace before, the King, and my Lady of Richmond bore the Queen's train." Richard's Queen was Anne, daughter of Warwick the Kingmaker. She had been betrothed to the Prince of Wales, who was treacherously slain, and according to repute by Richard himself, after the Battle of Tewkesbury. Through his first marriage she was sister-in-law to Lord Stanley.

By the end of that year, 1483, Stanley had been appointed " Constable of England for life," and restored to his old all-powerful office as Steward of the King's Household. As one of his biographers says, " Whatever happened to kings or to dynasties, it was the fate of Lord Stanley to flourish and increase."

Of all Lord Stanley's many changes of allegiance, his acceptance of office from Richard III., and his accompanying the usurper upon his progresses through the

country after his coronation, lays him most open to the adverse opinion and censure of history. He had openly proclaimed his loyalty to the boy-king Edward V., yet he had publicly acquiesced in Richard's theft of the crown! It is supposed that the terrible crime by which Richard made his usurpation secure—the murder of Edward V. and his brother, the little Duke of York, in the Tower of London—took place during one of these progresses. At any rate the two boys disappeared.

And now we come to a most curious incident, not only in the life of Lord Stanley, but in our history. It will be remembered that the Countess of Richmond had married as her second husband, Sir Henry Stafford, a younger son of Humphrey Stafford, Duke of Buckingham. When Richard III. seized the Crown of England, the dukedom of Buckingham was held by Humphrey Stafford's son, also called Humphrey, the nephew of the Countess of Richmond's second husband. This nephew was a strong partisan of Richard III., and like Lord Stanley, accompanied him upon his progress through the country. When they arrived at Gloucester, the young Duke took umbrage at what he considered a lack of proper regard on Richard's part for himself and his services and abruptly left the royal train, setting out with all speed for his Castle of Brecknock. Now Buckingham was directly descended from the seventh son of Edward III.—all the horrors and the troubles of the Wars of the Roses arose out of the descent of Lancastrians and Yorkists from that many-childrened monarch—and on the authority of Sir Thomas More, who was then a page at Brecknock Castle, we have it, that burning with rage and mortification, Buckingham, as he hurried towards Wales, conceived the idea of setting himself up as King and wresting the crown from the usurper Richard. But between Worcester and Bridgenorth he met the Countess of Richmond, his aunt by marriage, and Sir Thomas tells us that in the course of their conversation, she besought him, as being all-powerful with King Richard, to use his influence on behalf of her son, Henry of Richmond, still in exile in Brittany. All the Countess craved was that her son should be allowed to return and marry one of the daughters of Edward IV., whose only dowry should be the favour of Richard III. According to Sir Thomas More this request of the Countess set the Duke of Buckingham thinking, and by the time he arrived at Brecknock he had come to the conclusion that it would be more advantageous to him to support Henry of Richmond's claim to the throne in place of his own shadowy one. Richard III. had given the Duke the custody of Morton, Bishop of Ely, one of the supporters of Lord Hastings, and who had been arrested at the Council meeting in which Lord Stanley nearly lost his life. The Duke held the Bishop prisoner at Brecknock Castle, and burning with rage against Richard III., he confided to him his idea that Henry of Richmond should be King of England.

The Duke of Buckingham was a weak and foolish man, Margaret of Richmond was an astute woman. There is little doubt but in that interview by the roadside between Worcester and Bridgenorth she suggested some such arrangement in so subtle and veiled a manner—as only a clever woman can—that, as the idea germinated in his brain, the Duke was convinced it had originated with himself. Be that as it may, Bishop Morton strongly encouraged and supported the Duke, with the result that the two opened formal negotiations with the Countess of Rich-

mond. She had already sounded Queen Elizabeth Woodville as to the project of Henry of Richmond marrying one of her daughters; and being approached on this larger issue, the widowed Queen gladly welcomed the suggestion, and promised the co-operation of her friends. The murder of her sons, Edward V. and the Duke of York, in the Tower of London, was at this time being bruited abroad, and the distracted mother saw a ready means of vengeance upon Richard III And as word of the murder spread through the country, so the plot against the usurper thickened and widened. Great nobles and great ecclesiastics joined eagerly, providing money with a lavish hand. Messengers were dispatched to Henry of Richmond in Brittany with supplies and advice. He consented to every arrangement that was made by his mother and the others, and the 18th of October, 1483, was fixed for a general rising, it being settled that Henry should arrive in England before that date at the head of an armed force, in order to co-operate with the soldiers raised by Buckingham and the conspirators.

But stormy weather delayed Henry and scattered his ships, and when with one solitary vessel he attempted to land on the coast of Dorset, he found Richard's soldiery lining the beach. The Duke of Buckingham's rising had proved a failure, and he himself had been beheaded at Salisbury. Henry, therefore, had no choice but to return from whence he came.

All the time that the Countess of Richmond was plotting and arranging for this attack upon Richard, Lord Stanley was by the monarch's side, his most trusted councillor. Whilst the wife was the very spirit of the plot, the husband so managed matters that his own fidelity to the usurper could not be questioned. Yet

-R

Two days later (August 22) the battle took place, which put an end to the strife between Yorkist and Lancastrian, and made Henry Tudor, Earl of Richmond, King of England. In the very height of the battle, Sir William Stanley, Lord Stanley's brother, who was fighting for Richard, deserted him and joined forces with Henry. William Stanley's treachery gained Henry the day, but Lord Stanley was appointed Chancellor of the Exchequer and given the Order of the Garter, as well as estates and great riches.

Henry VII. married the daughter of Edward IV.—Elizabeth, the White Rose of York—and when their son, Prince Arthur, was born in 1486, the new Earl of Derby was one of the male sponsors. For ten years the two Stanley brothers were the greatest subjects in the land,

KNOWSLEY HALL

himself took no part in the action, "hanging between the two armies." Yet when all was over, and Richard lay amongst the slain, it was Lord Stanley who took the battered crown which had fallen from the usurper's helmet, and placed it on his step-son Henry Tudor's head.

Honours and lands were heaped upon the Stanley brothers. Lord Stanley was created Earl of Derby and given the forfeited estates of the Pilkingtons between Manchester and Bury. He also had " Pooton of Pooton's, Bythom of Bythom's, and Newby of Kirkby's estates in this county, with at least twenty gentlemen's estates more." Sir William Stanley and then the Perkin Warbeck insurrection sent Sir William to the scaffold and the grave. This Perkin Warbeck, who was a Fleming, gave himself out to be Richard, Duke of York, one of the sons of Edward IV., supposed to have been murdered in the Tower of London. His story was believed in Ireland and in Scotland, where the King, James IV., gave him his own cousin, Catherine Gordon, in marriage. Henry VII.'s secret inquiries satisfied him that Sir William Stanley was deeply concerned in the plot which supported Warbeck ; he was seized, tried, and condemned to death, and beheaded on February 14, 1495, his great wealth being forfeited to the King.

Henry VII. was notoriously avaricious, and it is thought that he allowed the extreme penalty to fall upon the man who had saved his cause at the Battle of Bosworth ten years previously, in order to become master of his estates and fortune. But Sir William was more impetuous than his calculating brother, and there is testimony that he did not cease to importune Henry for further honours in reward for his timely aid at Bosworth ; and so much so that Henry had begun to regard that service in another light. " The King's wit," says Francis Bacon, " began now to suggest unto his passion that Stanley at Bosworth Field, though he came time enough to save his life, yet he stayed long enough to endanger it."

The Earl of Derby was in no way com-promised in the affair of Perkin Warbeck, and so far from resenting or appearing to feel his brother's terrible end, in the summer of that year he received a state visit from Henry and his Queen of nearly a month's duration at Knowsley and at Lathom. The royal entertainment was upon the most magnificent scale, and it was only the Earl's fool who raised the shadow of the tragedy of the preceding February. Tradition has it that Henry VII. being taken on to the roof at Knowsley to see the view, the Earl of Derby's jester, who was present, seeing the King draw near to the edge of the leads which were unprotected by any balustrade, " stepped up to the Earl and pointing down the precipice said : ' Tom, remember Will !' "

Henry, it is said, understanding the

HENRY VII.
(From a contemporary bust by an Italian artist)

jester's meaning, "made all haste down the stairs and out of the house ; and the fool long after seemed mightily concerned that his lord had not the courage to take the opportunity of revenging himself for the death of his brother."

For Henry's convenience in crossing the Mersey Lord Derby built a bridge at Warrington, and thus deprived Sir John Butler, of Bewsey, of the emoluments of a ferry he held there. There arose a fierce quarrel, which resulted in the death of Sir John.[1]

Nine years after this visit Lord Derby died, at about the age of seventy, having retained the affection and regard of his royal step-son to the end. His wife survived him for five years. She was a remarkable woman, and, as has been described elsewhere in this work, was one of the first persons to found educational establishments in place of monasteries and

[1] See the "Legend of Bewsey Hall."

convents, being persuaded to this end by Hugh Oldham, a former protégé of hers, and the founder of the Manchester Grammar School.

"The first Stanley, Earl of Derby," says one of his biographers, "died full of years and honours, having survived the wars, executions, confiscations and multifarious perils of four reigns. All this presupposes great good fortune no doubt, but to have achieved such a career he must also have been a marvel of coolness, astuteness and dexterity. These are not qualities to be much admired when unaccompanied by others higher and nobler, yet their success on so great a scale excites a certain wonderment." Lord Derby certainly earned his reputation of "wily fox"; and he received the fullest reward for his genius in following the winning side, for at his death, "no lord in all the country was half so great a lord as he."

Old Liverpool 1889

You will find on the next 40 pages a reprint of a small booklet printed in 1889 to raise funds for St. Barnabas Church, Liverpool. The Author is the Rev. Richard Postance and the Artist, Mr. John Sanders. I have had the book many years and include it here as I hope, an enjoyable bonus.

Liverpool, Leverpool, Litherpoole, Lyverpoole, Lyrpole, Lerpool, Livrepol, Leverpole, — such are a few of the many ways in which the name of the good old Town has been turned and twisted. . As to the etymology of the word there is a great variety of opinion ; some deriving the first part of the word from a bird called the Liver, or Lever, or Laver; others from the word "lither" or lower , as distinguished from hireton or highertown (Everton); others from the word lithe, or bending, i.e. the bending-pool; others from the family name of Lever; others from a species of sea-weed (liverwort), found in the neighbourhood. From these and other derivations our readers may take any one they may choose. . As to the second portion of the name, we may reasonably suppose that "pool" means pool, though it is strange that the harbour and stream to which the town owes a part of its name, now no longer exist; they have passed away with nearly all the traces of Old Liverpool. The ancient water-course is sketched out on the first page. The first dock was made at the mouth of the pool at the beginning of the eighteenth century, and in 1826, according to the "Annals", the old dock was closed, to be filled up for the erection of the present Custom House and Post Office : since then there has been a marvellous development of the

LIVERPOOL 1650

Dock system, of which more later on.

The Tower of Liverpool, which stood at the bottom of Water Street (formerly called Bancke Street), has a strange eventful history, of which the earli--est part is very obscure. In the reign of Henry iv it seems to have come into the possession of Sir John Stanley, who in 1404 asked permission "to fortify his House at Leverpull." For many generations it remained as the sea-side stronghold of the Stanleys, and a convenient point of embarcation to their lordship in the Isle of Man, which was granted to Sir John after the battle of Shrewsbury. In 1532 we have accounts of Lord Derby maintaining 250 Liverpool residents, and feeding 60 old people daily, and entertaining visitors in the Tower three times weekly. During the siege of Liver--pool in 1644 the Tower was used as the head-quarters of the Parliamentarians, and after the surrender of the Town, Prince Rupert used both Tower and Castle for his soldiers and prisoners of war.

In 1737 the Tower passed into the hands of the Corporation of Liverpool, by whom it was converted into a Gaol for the imprisonment of war-prisoners, criminals, and debtors. It was however very ill-suited for the purpose, and very badly conducted : its cells were filthy and unwholesome, its surroundings close and unhealthy, and so lax was the discipline, that scenes of disorder and depravity were of frequent occurrence. John Howard, the philanthropist visited the place in 1775, and gave it a very bad character. He saw it again in 1779 and 1782, and although he found some improvement, he expressed his great satisfaction on hearing that the Corporation were contemplating the erection of a new Gaol.

TOWER OF LIVERPOOL.

121

The Tower was finally and completely demolished in 1819, and warehouses were erected on its site. In 1856 the warehouses were taken down, and the Offices, called "Tower Buildings", were constructed; so that of the old Liverpool Tower nothing but the name survives.

Passing from Water Street to Dale Street we come to a real old Liverpool thoroughfare, once very narrow, and more than once widened: it was irregularly built, and contained all sorts and conditions of houses, shops, taverns, and inns. It was one of the four principal Streets of the Town, proceeding from the "High Cross", which stood near the present Town Hall. The Crosses, one of the leading families of the place long ago, had a fine house in this Street, called the "Crosse Hall", with gardens extending to the Pool stream. Mr. Shaw, the potter, had his works and dwelling house at the corner of Fontenoy Street: after him was named old "Shaw's Brow", now so greatly changed since the erection of Brown's Library and Museum, and other buildings more recently added. Up to the year 1760 there was no coach road into Liverpool, but in that year, the new turnpike road to Prescot was completed (see map on the first page), and the first Stage-coach started with passengers from the "Golden Fleece" in Dale Street. Previous to that date, goods were carried by Canal and on horse-back, and long lines of pack-horses, laden with goods, issued forth periodically from Dale Street to the interior. Passengers to London had to take horse and make their way to Warrington, whence coaches started twice a week to the Metropolis, occupying three days on the journey; the fare was two guineas. The coaches which afterwards started from Liverpool, ran through to London, making the journey generally in two days in summer, and three days in winter, leaving the "Golden Fleece" on the mornings of Tuesday and Friday. Passengers very frequently carried arms, so as to be

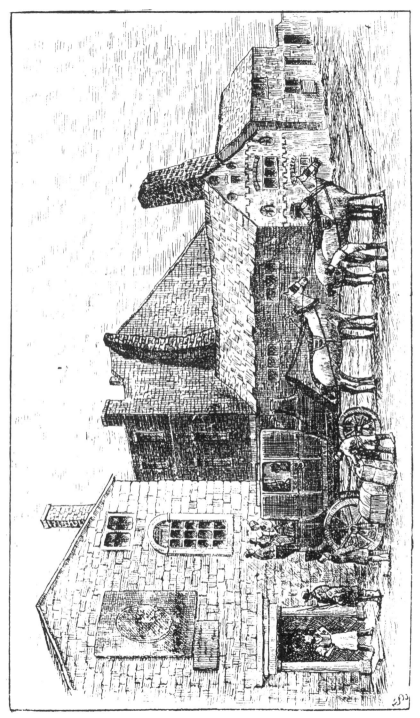

DALE STREET

123

prepared for possible highwaymen. Other inns in Dale Street were the "Golden Lion", the "Angel and Crown", the "Bull and Punch-bowl", the "Wool-pack", and the "Red Lion".

Lime Street, which, at the beginning of this century, was literally nowhere, has, since the opening of Lime St. Station, the building of St George's Hall and other noble edifices, been transformed into one of the busiest and finest thoroughfares in the Provinces. In old days it was the scene of much disorder and brutality, as it was the resort of the roughs of the town for cock-fighting, dog-fighting, and prize-fighting. It was once called "Limekiln Lane", from the lime-works which stood on the site of the Railway Station. The fumes from these works were supposed to be prejudicial to the patients in the old Infirmary, and the kilns were removed to the North Shore. The Infirmary, erected in 1745, stood on part of the land now occupied by St. George's Hall. There were rope-walks between Lime St. and Clayton Square, and on the east side of the Street, rope-walks and wind-mills. The Blind Asylum and Church were erected at the London Road end, but as the land on which the Church stood, was required for the enlargement of the Station in 1850, the whole Institution was re-built in Hardman Street, the Church itself being removed and re-erected stone by stone. When the Liverpool and Manchester Railway was first opened, the terminus was in Crown Street, and passengers were brought in and out of Town by coach: in 1836 the tunnel was completed, and the Station opened: since then the Station has been improved, enlarged and re-built, and the old Station front has given place to the North-Western Hotel. St John's Churchyard was consecrated as a cemetery in 1767, though St. John's Church was not completed till 1784. It is now entirely overshadowed by St George's Hall. The first stone of this majestic Hall was laid on the coronation day of Queen Victoria, June 28, 1838, and was opened Sept. 12. 1854.

VIEW from LIME STREET

125

Lord Street was at one time a portion of the orchard belonging to the Castle, which stood upon the ground now occupied by St. George's Church:(see picture and descrip-tion of the Castle). A lane ran through the orchard, leading to a ferry across the pool stream which flowed from the Moss Lake Fields, and after a circuitous route, made its way to the river via Byrom St., Whitechapel (formerly called Frog Lane), Paradise St., and the Custom House. There were a few cottages in Lord Lane, occupied by some of the Castle retainers. During the siege (1644), these few houses were near-ly all demolished, and buildings of a better class were erect--ed. In 1672 Lord Molyneux constructed a bridge over the pool at the bottom of Lord St, (then called Lord Molyneux Street). The Molyneux family built a mansion on the site of the present Commerce Court, when the Castle was no longer habitable. The Street itself, like all the old streets, was exceedingly narrow, two carriages could scarcely pass, and indeed in those old days of sedan chairs, carriages were very few; no Street open-ed into Lord St throughout its whole length till 1777, when John St. was opened out from Harrington St., and was continued across the road into Cable St. Lord St., towards the end of the last century gradually developed into a very important thorough--fare, as the Town extended eastward; consequently the narrow--ness of the Street was a very great drawback to business and traffic, and in 1826 an Act was obtained for increasing its width fourfold : this, and other improvements in the im--mediate neighbourhood, were carried out at a cost of about £170,000.

Church Street increased in importance with Lord St. The Church which gave it its name, was consecrated in 1704, Liverpool having become a Parish, separate from Walton, in 1699. St. Peter's was a second Parish Church, and a second Rector was appointed, the living being in the gift of the coun-cil. This arrangement was subsequently altered, the advowson

LORD STREET

was sold by the Corporation in 1838, and not long afterwards there was but one Rector for the two Parish Churches. The Blue-Coat School was founded in 1709, and in a house next to it, the first Milner's safes were manufactured. Church St. was paved in 1760, and the side-walks flagged in 1816. Bold Street was built upon in 1785, but for many years contained only private houses.

Castle Street is one of the old Liverpool streets, and owing to its central position, between the old Castle and the old High Cross, it has been the scene of very many of the most important events in the history of the old town. It was of course very narrow at one time, about the width of Cable St., and was widened in 1786. The market for corn and other produce used to be held under the old Town Hall which was built upon arches. When the Castle was demolished, the market was held in the open space called Derby Square; but as the business of the town increased, and the market in Castle St. became very inconvenient, St John's Market was built, and opened in 1822. St James' Market was built in 1827. The first Liverpool newspapers were published in Castle St, namely "Williamson's Liverpool Advertiser", which appeared on May 28, 1756, and Gore's "General Advertiser", first published in 1765. There was however according to "Brooke's Ancient Liverpool", a newspaper called the "Liverpoole Courant", published as early as 1712. Gore's Liverpool Directory was first issued in 1766, and has been continued ever since, growing in size with the increasing population.   Brunswick Street was opened out in 1790; it is the centre of the Liverpool corn trade, which was carried on opposite the Town Hall until 1803: the Corn Exchange was erected soon afterwards, but greatly increased trade necessitated larger premises, and the new Corn Exchange was opened in 1854. St. George's Church, at the south end of Castle St, was built in 1734, on the site of the Castle, it has however been almost entirely re-built.

CASTLE STREET

St. Nicholas' Church, which used to be called the "Church of Our Lady and St Nicholas", bears the very appropriate title of "the Old Church". The original structure was a chapel of ease to the mother Church at Walton until Liverpool was made a separate Parish in 1699. The Church has from time to time been subjected to many alterations, improvements, and re-constructions, and the Church-yard, as we all know, has not been left intact, since the filling up of the George's Dock Basin and the carrying out of other improvements. In 1725 a new peal of six bells, cast in Bristol, was put up in the tower; this peal was however superseded by a very fine set of twelve bells, which were cast in 1813. In 1750 the old tower had a new spire erected upon it, and in 1774 the body of the Church was re-built. On Sunday, Feb 11, 1810, a deplorable calamity happened: the spire, which had been built upon the old tower, fell into the Church, just as the children of the Moorfields Charity School were proceeding up the aisle. Twenty children and three adults were killed upon the spot, and many others injured: the Rector and his Curate, who were entering the Church at the time, had a most miraculous escape. In 1815 the present lantern tower was erected. Some curious inscriptions have been traced in the Church-yard: one tombstone records the death of one Robert Broadneux, who died aged 109 years: he lay down to die when upwards of four score years old, and had his coffin made, but as he lived on for more than a quarter of a century, the ghastly piece of furniture was kept in his bed-room until his death. Another tombstone to the memory of Richard Blore, 1789, moralizes thus: —

"This town's a corporation full of crooked streets,
"Death is the market-place, where all men meets:
"If life was merchandise that men could buy:
"The rich would always live, the poor would die."

ANCIENT PARISH CHURCH OF LIVERPOOL;

THE Customs' duties of Liverpool used to be received at the old Town Hall in High Street, and when this building was taken down in 1675, the old Custom House was erected at the bottom of Water Street, on the opposite side to the Tower, a space being left between the river and Custom House for the reception of merchandise. The river in those days, before the reclaiming of land for Docks and Quays, flowed right up to St. Nicholas' Church Yard, to the foot of the present Tower Buildings, and the east side of the back Goree. This old Custom House was a curious little place, more like a fisherman's cottage than a public building, but it served its purpose for a few years, and remained standing until about 1780, when the Goree warehouses were erected on its site. These warehouses were destroyed by a terrible conflagration in 1802, great clouds of smoke and sparks being carried for miles across the country: the fire smouldered, it is said, for three months, and the amount of loss was estimated at £323,000.

When the little cottage Custom House was found to be too small and inconvenient for the increasing business of the port, a more suitable building was chosen and adapted for the purpose on the quay of the new Dock, afterwards called the Custom House Dock, and subsequently the "Old Dock". The building belonged to Sylvester Moorcroft, (who was Mayor in 1706), and stood on the east side of the Dock, near the site of the Sailors' Home. It was a neat brick building faced with stone, and with the Royal arms carved in stone in front: there was a flight of steps at the entrance, which led to an open lobby or piazza, above which was the "long room" for the transaction of Customs' business; behind the building was a spacious yard with suitable warehouses. This Custom House was pulled down in 1837—a side view of it is seen in the picture of the "Old Dock". The present Custom House occupies

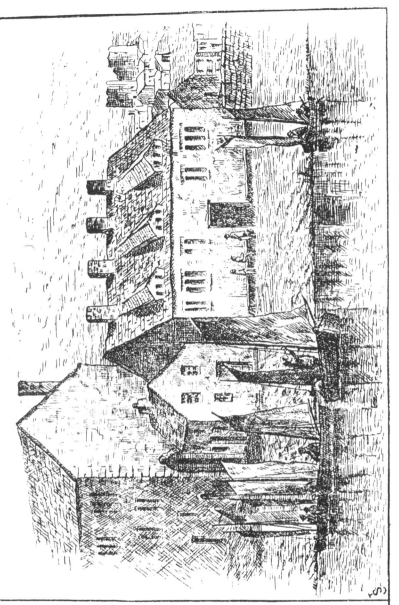

OLD CUSTOM HOUSE.

the site of the "Old Dock", which was filled up for the
purpose. This noble pile of buildings consists of a centre
surmounted by a dome, on either side of which are two
extensive wings, in which are various departments in
connection with the Excise, Dock estate, and Post Office, the
latter having been removed from "Post-office Place", Church St.

Park Lane was formerly a horse-road, leading to Toxteth Park and commenced at the ferry at the foot of South Castle Street, then called Water Lane; a hundred years ago there were no houses in or about Blundell Street; Norfolk Street terminated at Simpson Street, and from there, beautiful green fields sloped down to the South Shore! A mill and dam stood near the bottom of Stanhope Street, quite in the open country. Toxteth Park, now so densely populated, was in the early part of the present century, entirely agricultural, a few houses, farm dwellings, market-gardeners' cottages, etc. were scattered over the landscape, through which ran the Park Road to Aigburth and Garston. Not far from St. James' Church, which was built in 1774-1775, was the great quarry between Parliament Street and Duke Street, from which the stone was obtained for many of the Public Buildings of Liverpool. In 1829 the quarry became St James' Cemetery, where, in the following year, were laid the mortal remains of the Right honourable William Huskisson, M.P. for the Borough, who met with a fatal accident, at the opening of the Liverpool and Manchester Railway, Sept.15 1830. Near where the Cemetery Chapel now stands, was an old windmill, and two others stood at the Parliament Street end of the quarry. Flowing from the rock on the east side a little spring of water was discovered, which has ever since been supposed to contain valuable medi- -cinal properties. St. James' Mount was constructed in 1767: it was the outcome of the benevolence of a Mr. Thomas Johnson, Mayor of Liverpool at the time, who, during a winter of terrible severity, relieved the dis- -tress of the people, by employing large numbers of men to form this artificial hill, and to lay out the Mount Gardens. This promenade originally went by the name of "Mount Zion."

MILL & QUARRY [S⋅ JAMES MOUNT]

Near the highest part of Park Road stood an old road-side Inn, a quaint-looking structure, with an unknown history and of uncertain age, which bore the name of the "Peacock Tavern". Further along the road was the "Pine Apple Tavern and Bowling-Green", which many will remember as the terminus of a line of omnibuses, and a favourite place of resort. It was originally a farm-house, with farm lands of very considerable dimensions, but now streets of small dwelling-house property are built upon its acres, and this portion of old Toxteth Park is fast losing every trace of the picturesque. "The Peacock" and "The Pine Apple" are no more — they have fallen before the devastating march of population to the South, just as northward the once beautiful and aristocratic Everton, the "Clifton" of Liverpool, with its fine suburban residences, its old fashioned row of cottages and the renowned Toffee Shop on the Brow, has been transformed into a densely peopled district, extending to Walton Church and beyond it.

At the extreme end of Park Road stands a plain stone building, with graveyard attached, called the Ancient Chapel of Toxteth Park. Although never regularly consecrated, it is said to have been at one time used by a Church of England congregation. In the time of Cromwell it was a Dissenting Place of Worship, and after the Restoration it was not affected by the Act of Uniformity, but continued to be occupied by Nonconformists. It was re-built in 1774, and in 1777 a secession took place, owing to dissatisfaction at the appointment of a Minister of unorthodox views: this led to the erection of Newington Chapel in Renshaw Street,

EVERTON TOFFEE SHOP [BROW SIDE.]

PEACOCK INN [PARK ROAD]

now used as the German Church. In the year 1811 a very remarkable man was appointed to the pastorate of Newington Chapel, the Rev. Thomas Spencer, who was born in 1791; his popularity as a preacher was so great that a larger Chapel had to be found to accommodate the crowds who flocked to hear him, and Great George Street Chapel was forthwith commenced. Unfortunately however Mr Spencer was drowned whilst bathing, before the building was completed, and thus a most promising career was cut short at its very outset. The Rev.Thomas Raffles (afterwards D.D) succeeded him, and so marked was the esteem in which he was held as a preacher and public man for fifty years, that his name will always be remembered amongst the great and good men of our City, and the Chapel in which he ministered so long and so faithfully, will probably be known for many years to come by the name which has by common consent been given to it for many years past – "Raffles' Chapel". The Ancient Chapel of Toxteth, from which this congregation originally seceded, has been since used by the Unitarian Body.

But to return to old Liverpool – to the very centre of commercial activity – the place where merchants most do congregate. The Town Hall, which was commenced in 1748 was intended to answer the double purpose of a Town Hall and Exchange, but the merchants chose to transact their business in the open air, and met at the end of Castle Street, opposite "Gore's", now Mawdesley's, where they held "High Change". From all accounts it seems that the old dome of the Town Hall was not an elegant structure, and was destroyed by fire, with the interior of the building, on Sunday, Jan. 18. 1795,

the destruction being all the more complete in consequence of the scarcity of water owing to the frost. The work of restoration was promptly and rapidly proceeded with, the interior was re-arranged, the new dome and the figure of Britannia were put up in 1802, and the portico in the

front was added in 1811, the pillars of the latter are
each of one stone, obtained not from the great quarry in
St James' Road, but from a fine quarry of excellent
stone, on the east side of Rathbone Street; the great rough-
-hewn blocks were carried down to Castle Street, where
they were shaped and dressed. The splendid suite of
State apartments and the ball-room were completed in
1820. While, however, the new Town Hall was sufficiently
commodious, elegant, and suitable for its purpose, the
necessity for a new Exchange became more and more
pressing, and the "Exchange Buildings Scheme" was project-
-ed, the shares were rapidly taken up, and in 1808 the
merchants assembled on the "flags" at the rear of the
newly-restored Town Hall, and forsook their old place of
meeting in Castle Street. The Nelson monument, with
the well-known motto "England expects every man to do
his duty", was erected directly after the decisive victory
of Trafalgar, and the death of Admiral Lord Nelson.
For little more than fifty years these old Exchange
Buildings were found sufficient for the business men
of Liverpool : in the mean time, however, commercial
enterprise had not been at a stand-still ; rapid progress
and development were the order of the day, and new
Exchange Buildings were regarded as a necessity.
In 1862 a new Exchange Company was formed, to buy
up the old Company, and to erect the present magnifi-
-cent series of business premises and the spacious
News-room. Although from an architectural point of
view, there are many who profess a preference for the
old Exchange, yet it must be admitted that few of the
world's Market-places can compare with the Court-yard
of our Town Hall, where day by day is to be seen the
concentration of the marvellous business enterprise
and activity of the City of Liverpool.

EXCHANGE BUILDINGS (CHAPEL S?)

TO write the history of the Liverpool Docks would be to tell the whole story of the rise and progress of the town. As, however, it is impossible here to give an account of all the Docks, it may be interesting to notice the oldest, and to refer to some of the newest. As long ago as 1561 a shelter for the shipping, consisting of massive stone piers, was erected at the mouth of the pool; but it was not until 1709 that the first Dock Act was passed: soon afterwards, the first Liverpool Dock (and in fact, the first in the kingdom) was completed: it was 195 yards long, with an irregular width of 80 to 95 yards. In 1826 it was filled up to make a site for the new Revenue Buildings. The Salthouse Dock, so called from the salt works on the east side of it, was opened in 1753, it was originally called the South Dock. The next was the George's, or North Dock, which was commenced in 1762 and opened in 1771. It was enlarged and almost entirely re-constructed early in the present century, and re-opened in 1825. The George's pier and slip was the point of arrival and departure of various packets and ferry boats.

Rapidly increasing trade soon demanded further accommodation, and an Act was passed in 1785 authorizing the construction of two more Docks, south of the Salthouse, called the King's (opened 1788), and the Queen's (opened 1796). Both these Docks have been since re-constructed and enlarged. The King's Dock tobacco warehouse was erected in 1795 on the east side, but afterwards very much larger warehouses were built on the west side. The Prince's Dock was opened, July 19, 1821, the coronation day of George iv. The Dock Estate then extended gradually north and south. The last important Act was obtained in 1873, to meet the requirements of steam-ships of vastly increased size and tonnage; the estimate for these new schemes being £4,100,000. The new Docks at the north end comprised the Langton half-tide, two graving-docks, the Langton Branch, the Alexandra and its three branches,

OLD DOCK AND CUSTOM HOUSE

and the Hornby Dock. This extensive addition to the Dock accommodation was opened by the Prince and Princess of Wales on Sept.8. 1881. The new works at the South end included the enlargement of the Hercula-neum Dock, with its graving-docks, and the completion of the whole series between the Brunswick Dock and the Dingle. There are in Liverpool sixty docks and basins, with a water area of 360 acres, length of quay berthing 25 miles and a frontage to the river of more than six miles. The number of graving-docks belonging to the Board is 21 ; and the total area of the Estate is 1078 acres. The Liverpool Estate also extends to the Birkenhead side, the docks there, in an incomplete state, having been purchased and finished by the Liverpool Dock Board. This portion of the Estate comprises an area of 506 acres, with water space of 164½ acres, and a lineal quayage of over 9 miles. There are 3 graving-docks on this side belonging to the Board. [Much of the above information has been gathered from a paper by G.F. Lyster Esq (Dock Engineer), which was kindly placed at the disposal of the writer of these pages.]

In the year in which the first Dock Act was passed, 1709, the Blue-Coat Hospital was founded by Mr. Bryan Blundell, who gave large sums of money at various times, for the benefit of this charity, in which he and his family took so deep and lasting an interest. At first it was only a day charity school, but it was soon found desirable to enlarge its scope, to undertake the entire care of the children, and to take a kindly interest in them in after life. The present building was erected in 1717, but it has since been much altered and improved : the front facing School Lane presents much the same appearance as it originally did. The Sunday afternoon Service in the Chapel, to which the public are admitted, is of a most interesting character, and is sufficient evidence in itself

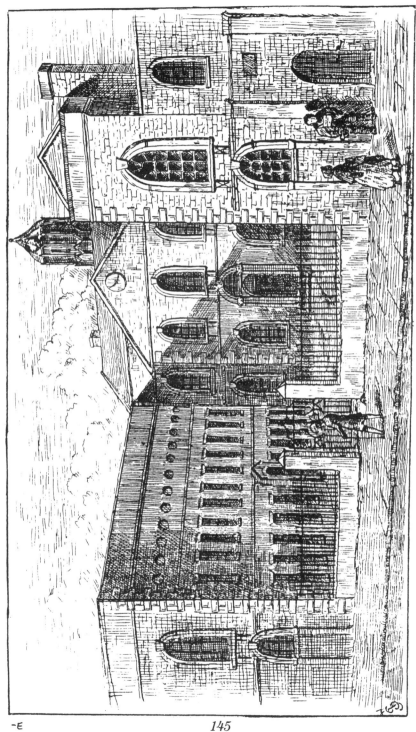

BLUE COAT HOSPITAL

of the thoroughness of the instruction given, and the excellent discipline maintained.

Liverpool Castle is generally supposed to have been built by Roger de Poictiers about the year 1080, though in "Picton's Memorials" we find this surmise contradicted on what appear to be very reasonable grounds, and the opinion is expressed that "the Castle was built by King John, at the time when he founded the borough and port," (about 1206). The Castle occupied the site of St George's Church, but covered a much larger area, embracing the open space at the top of Lord St., it was surrounded by strong battlemented walls, with four round towers with battlements: the principal entrance was on the north side facing Castle St, a tower being on each side, and a drawbridge to the gate. The whole fortification was enclosed within a wide and deep fosse or moat, cut in the solid rock round the Castle. Portions of the foundations of the towers, and parts of the moat, have been discovered, at various times, in making excavations for buildings. In 1421 Sir Richard Molyneux of Sefton was made Constable of the Castle, and the office remained hereditary in the family. The building sustained some injury during the siege in 1644, and was captured and occupied by Prince Rupert, who approached it by way of Castle St. Shortly afterwards an Act was passed for the demolition of the Castle; but this was not immediately done, as later on it was used as a residence, and afterwards degenerated into a refuge for idle persons, who became a nuisance and were ejected by the Corporation; a portion of it was also used as a bridewell. When Liverpool was made a separate Parish in 1699, and two Rectors were appointed, it seems they took up their abode within the Castle walls, and refused to "surrender" to the Corporation. They gave up possession however in 1715, and the Corporation agreed to build two houses for them by way of compensation. The walls and ruins of the dismant- led Castle were pulled down and removed in 1721.

LIVERPOOL CASTLE.

A hundred years ago, "crossing the water" was a serious and risky undertaking; the ferry boats for the accommodation of passengers were small and inconvenient, and the ferry houses were quite in keeping with them. There were ferries at Woodside, Lower Tranmere, Seacombe, Rock Ferry, New Ferry, & Eastham, and the most usual place for landing on the Liverpool side was the George's pier. Passengers were conveyed in small boats of five or six tons burden, with accommodation for about fifteen people, and it is easy to imagine that in boisterous weather, and with a strong tide running, the voyage was at times a perilous one. The first steam ferry-boat to cross the Mersey was a strange looking craft called the "Etna", which commenced to run in 1817. It was a kind of double boat, with one paddle-wheel in the middle. Although this vessel was a great advance upon the old ferry boats, the dangers of embarking & landing passengers were not diminished, as at low tide the steamer could not come alongside the steps, and small boats had to be used. This dangerous and inconvenient landing was a source of frequent complaints, and at length a "gut" was made, into which the steamers ran and landed their passengers on a slip, which was only a little less disagreeable than the steps, and accidents, more or less serious, were of frequent occurrence. The next move was the construction of a small stage running in and out of a tunnel according to the state of the tide. This landing stage difficulty was at length solved by the building of the George's floating stage in 1847 by the Dock Board at a cost of £60,000; it was 500 feet long and 80 feet wide. The rapid increase of traffic, and the necessity of further accommodation for all kinds of passenger steamers led to the construction of the Prince's Landing-stage by the Dock Board, at a cost of £120,000, it was 1002 feet long and 80 feet wide. The stages were connected with the quays of the river wall by means of hinged girder bridges, so as to rise and fall with the tide.

SEACOMBE FERRY SLIP

WOODSIDE FERRY SLIP

149

The two landing-stages were united in 1873-4, and formed a magnificent promenade deck, 2060 feet in length; the total cost of the whole structure, with the improved bridges and approaches, being £373,000. Shortly after its completion, it was, to every ones amazement, destroyed by fire, July 28, 1874. The fire originated beneath the flooring, where some men were at work, and owing to the highly inflammable nature of the timber which had been saturated with creosote, the efforts of the firemen were absolutely useless: the fire could not be reached, and nearly every portion of the stage was ruined, the loss being about £250,000. The work of re--construction was soon proceeded with, and the Landing-stage was, in a very short time, once more ready for its enormous traffic.

On the page opposite is a view in London Road; this is comparatively a modern Street, although it was one of the ancient ways out of Liverpool. It used to be called "the way to Warrington", and was traversed by strings of pack-horses, as up to the middle of the last century there was no coach road out of Liverpool, the nearest coach town being Warring-ton. (see Dale St.) As soon as the road was made, and the coaches ran through to Liverpool, London Road became an important and crowded thoroughfare. In the early part of the present century there were no houses between the corner of Stafford Street and Commutation Row; at the corner of Norton Street stood the old "Blue Bell Inn", a recognized stopping place for the Liverpool coaches. In and near this locality several traces have been discovered of the entrenchments and other military works and relics connected with the celebrated siege of Liverpool by Prince Rupert, who took the Town by assault, June, 1664. One of the most conspicuous objects in the neighbourhood is the Statue of King George iii, which was erected by public subscription, though funds did not come in as readily as could be desired. The first stone

LONDON ROAD.

for the pedestal was laid in Great George Square garden on Oct. 25th 1809, being the fiftieth anniversary of King George's accession to the throne. In 1822 it was decided to alter the site to London Road, and there the figure was set up, but the monument was not completed until the following year.

We are drawing near to the end of our short story, and yet how much there is to tell! So many and so great are the changes through which Liverpool has passed since those early days in her history when the "Pool" was her harbour and the Castle her most prominent feature, since the "High Cross" stood in her Market-place, and the "White Cross" at the corner of Oldhall Street; since the "Everton Cross", which took the form of a sun-dial, stood at the top of the town in a line with Everton Road; since the Everton Beacon Tower held its commanding position where St. George's Church now stands; since the "stocks" stood in front of St. Peter's Church, and by the old Parish Church of Walton. Since those days Liverpool has extended far away north, south, and east; there are now houses, houses, everywhere, even where but a very few years ago, we used to take our walks abroad into the country, through fields and lanes and villages. Fortunately for the people, the town is not without its "lungs"; but the crowded state of the Parks, especially during the summer months, is evidence enough that they are neither too many nor too large : they are more-over a considerable distance from the great mass of the town-toilers, who have to be content with the relief and refreshment afforded by the carefully tended green of a few squares and grave-yards. In fact the greater part of Liverpool is painfully new, and to hear her called the "good old town" sounds something like a misnomer. The relics of "Old Liverpool" are being

SUN DIAL

OLD CROSS

STOCKS

BEACON

gradually crowded out, and at the present rate of the process of destruction, the time is not far distant when the antiquarian will have to depend entirely upon books and pictures for the objects of his research. Many and great changes have taken place in Liverpool ancient and modern: what further changes may take place it is difficult to prophesy

let us hope, however, that all changes will be for her
greater prosperity, and the welfare of her people. Without
doubt there is at the present time a strong tendency in
favour of more light, more room, more air for the people,
and more facilities for all manner of physical, mental,
and moral improvement. May the best hopes of her
True sons be realized!

ON the opposite page is a view familiar to all
Liverpool people - it is the Liverpool of to-day. Were all
its history told, it would be a strange story of profit and
loss, success and disaster, wealth and poverty, virtue and
vice, philanthropy and degradation, culture and ignorance,
religious activity and heathendom. Truly Liverpool has
much wherein she may rejoice, but much cause also for
shame and humiliation. She has been named the "black
spot on the Mersey", and though this evil repute is not
the result altogether of her own black deeds, but rather
from the fact of her being "the meeting-place of the
nations", yet it is greatly to be desired that this reproach
should be for ever rolled away. Our desire in preparing
the foregoing pages has been simply to gather together
a few facts in a small compass, which may be useful
and interesting to Liverpool people especially, and to
give some idea of the old buildings which have been
swept away by modern enterprise and progress.
Apology is offered, if need be, for the informal and
gossiping manner in which the information is given,
we hope that inaccuracies will not be found very
numerous, and that many readers, for whom the
more complete and costly works on the subject are
difficult of access, may derive pleasure and profit
from the perusal of this little work on

"Old Liverpool."

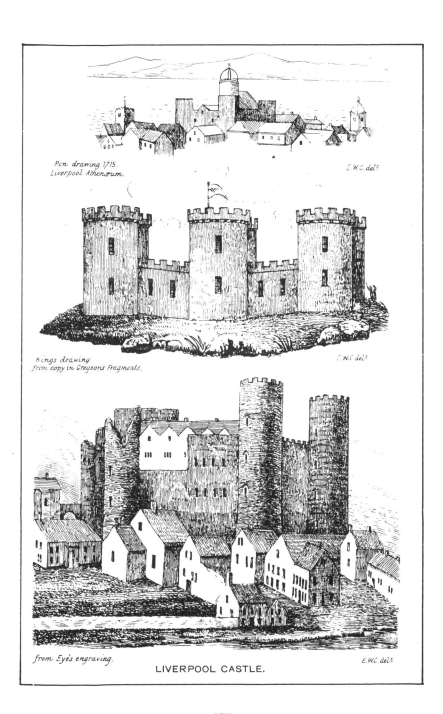

Pen drawing 1715.
Liverpool Athenæum.

E.W.C. delt

Kings drawing.
from copy in Greysons Fragments.

E.W.C delt

from Eye's engraving.

E.W.C delt

LIVERPOOL CASTLE.

155

Liverpool Castle (17th century)

Restored from authentic plans and measurements by Edward W. Cox.

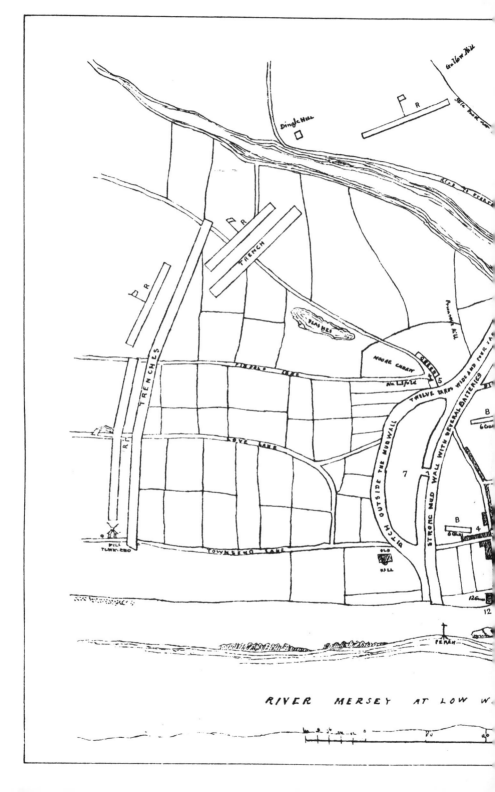

RIVER MERSEY AT LOW W.

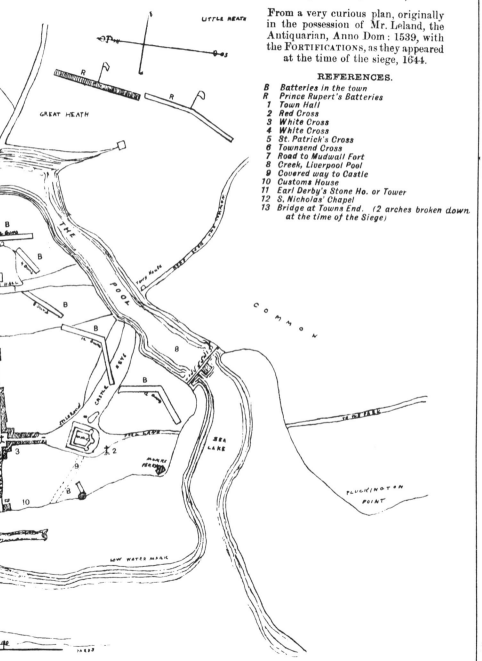

HISTORICAL MAP OF LIVERPOOL

(Facsimile, reduced)

From a very curious plan, originally in the possession of Mr. Leland, the Antiquarian, Anno Dom : 1539, with the FORTIFICATIONS, as they appeared at the time of the siege, 1644.

REFERENCES.

B   Batteries in the town
R   Prince Rupert's Batteries
1   Town Hall
2   Red Cross
3   White Cross
4   White Cross
5   St. Patrick's Cross
6   Townsend Cross
7   Road to Mudwall Fort
8   Creek, Liverpool Pool
9   Covered way to Castle
10   Customs House
11   Earl Derby's Stone Ho. or Tower
12   S. Nicholas' Chapel
13   Bridge at Towns End. (2 arches broken down at the time of the Siege)

N. Gregson direx

"This Plate was Engraved as a present for Mr. John Hely intended History of Liverpool."

TOWER AT LIVERPOOL,

Built in 1406 by Sir John Stanley, Kn.t

N. Johnson del. & sculp.t Liverpool.

Pictures of Olde Liverpool

THESE GEMS REVIVIFYING OLD DAYS AND SCENES
HAVE BEEN SELECTED BY THE PERMISSION
OF THE LIBRARIES COMMITTEE OF
THE CITY OF LIVERPOOL

ORIGINALLY PRINTED & PUBLISHED BY
THE DAILY POST PRINTERS
LIVERPOOL

OLD CUSTOM HOUSE AND CASTLE, 1650

On the left is a portion of the Tower (across the street, Water
Street, the house of Captain Dawson). The building in the
centre (cart by the door) is the Custom House of the period and
the third erected in the Town. In the distance the Castle.

THE TOWER OF LIVERPOOL, 1680

The Tower of Liverpool, foot of Water Street, erected late in the
thirteenth century.   Fortified in 1404, demolished in 1819.   A
view from the river showing, also, old St. Nicholas' Church.

CASTLE OF LIVERPOOL, 1689

With the Castle of Liverpool and its surrounding dependencies, the nucleus of the town begins. The Castle contained the numerous buildings necessary for a garrison, with cultivated grounds, extending to the Pool at the bottom of Lord Street and embracing the space now occupied by Lord Street, Harrington Street and the North end of Castle Street. In 1689 when the Army of William III arrived, although the Castle was hastening to decay, it was still serviceable to troops, the regiment entering is the seventeenth foot. In the year 1704 the Corporation rented the Castle for £6/13/4 per annum.

OLD CUSTOM HOUSE AND OLD DOCK, 1760

On the left the fourth Custom House, Old Dock (from Trafford
Wient), which stood on the site of the Arcade near the Sailors'
Home.   This Dock was the first constructed in Liverpool—the
picture shows the east end.   The Spire of St. Thomas' Church
(erected in 1750) is seen in the background.

OLD DOCK, 1809

Entrance to the Dock, looking North, showing the spires of St.
Nicholas' Church and St. George's Church, Strand Street
approach, Dock Step, Marshall Lane, and one side of the street
called " Dry Dock."

MANN ISLAND

South side, between Nova Scotia and Irwell Street at foot of
James Street, viewed from South East corner of Old George's
Dock.

SECOND TOWN HALL AND EXCHANGE

Described as "A Famous Town House," placed on pillars and
arches of hewn stone and had underneath the Public Exchange
for Merchants. It stood about the centre of Castle Street.
Erected 1673; demolished 1754-5. View shows adjoining
shops in Castle Street looking to High Street.

CASTLE DITCH, 1756

The shops present a very humble appearance compared to our
present shop magnificence, yet they were tenanted by the first
tradesmen of that time. In the centre Lord Street, showing
St. Peter's Church in the background. This site is partially
covered by St. George's Crescent.

CASTLE STREET, 1786

Looking South, showing demolition of West side for widening
purposes. This view is as seen from site of present Town Hall.
About the middle, on the left-hand side, is the principal hotel
at this time, called the Queen's Arms, and used as the Assembly
Rooms of the town.   Since the foundation of Liverpool in 1076,
Castle Street has been the site of almost every scene of interest
that has occurred.

CHAPEL STREET, 1797

The buildings appear to be principally mansions—the residences
of Merchants who had their places of business close by. The
view represents the street from the corner of Old Hall Street to
Bath Street.

LANCELOT'S HEY

Was the first opening from Chapel Street northwards, in 1650,
it was a field called Lancelot's Croft. The cottages are interesting specimens of early thatched houses and show the date of
their erection, 1674.

JAMES STREET

James Street takes its name from an old Liverpool family and was partly built in 1680—one of the earliest streets of the town. The old fish market, built in 1791, was on the right, it extended through Fenwick Street and part of the way down Moor Street. It was demolished in 1839.

POOL LANE, 1798

The old shambles at the top of Pool Lane (now South Castle
Street) which remained until 1820.   The principal market was
held in the open space in the vicinity.   The street to the right is
Redcross Street.   Pool Lane (formerly Water Lane) was originally a sandy lane outside the town.

REDCROSS STREET

A portion of the South side of the street. The principal white house was originally a stone house, the home of some of the early merchants of the town. The archway is now called Mercer's Court.

BROW SIDE, EVERTON

Where "Everton Toffee" was made and sold. The Round
House is shown in the centre of the picture on the steep plot of
grass.